Abou

Tim Wright is the co-host of the *Wonder of Parenting Podcast: A Brain-Science Approach to Parenting.* He and his wife Jan have two adult children and five grandchildren. They live in Glendale, AZ, where Tim enjoys his daily recumbent bike rides and lives for the day when the Arizona Cardinals win the Supe… the Big Game. He and Jan also enjoy sitting on the beach in Maui watching the whales.

Aloha RiverHome: The GOOD Prophecy is his third book in *The Adventures of Toby Baxter* series.

http://www.TimWrightBooks.com

Praise for Aloha RiverHome: The GOOD Prophecy

In *The GOOD Prophecy,* Tim Wright delivers an exhilarating blend of fantasy and adventure that captivates readers from the get-go and holds a spell on them that persists until the final page... This entry into the series delivers, in every aspect, a gorgeous treat for fans of adventure and fantasy with intriguing characters and strong plot points.—**The Book Commentary**

Toby's adventure is altogether thrilling, wholesome, fun, and extraordinary. It's highly engaging for kids, teens, and adults. And with its unforgettably witty banter and fast-paced fantastical plot, it's sure to leave readers endlessly entertained!—**Chick Lit Café**

The Adventures of Toby Baxter Book 3: Aloha RiverHome: The GOOD Prophecy is a thrilling and thought-provoking addition to the series that will captivate readers of all ages. Tim Wright's imaginative storytelling, richly drawn characters, and vivid world-building combine to create an immersive reading experience that will leave readers eagerly awaiting the next chapter in Toby's journey.—**readingwithyourkids.com**

Don't waste your time on this book. Author is a terrible writer and Toddy Boxcar isn't worth it!—@chieftainPlythar. **InstaTroll Reviews**

The Adventures Of Toby Baxter
Book 3

Aloha RiverHome:
The GOOD Prophecy

Tim Wright

The Adventures Of Toby Baxter
Book 3

Books in the series:

Book 1: The River Elf, the Giant, and the Closet

Book 2: RiverHome for the Holidays

Book 3: Aloha RiverHome: The GOOD Prophecy

Free Prequels

Book 1 Prequel: *I.C.E. Call Toby Baxter*

Book 2 Prequel: *'Twas the Night Before RiverHome*

Book 3 Prequel: *Not So Good In RiverHome*

Join the mailing list to receive the free prequels:

https://timwrightbooks.substack.com/

Copyright ©Tim Wright, 2024. All rights reserved. No part of this publication may be reproduced, stored, or transmitted in any form or by any means, electronic, mechanical, photocopying, recording, or scanning, or otherwise without written permission from Tim Wright. It is illegal to copy this book, post it to a website, or distribute it by any other means without permission.

This is a work of fiction. Names, characters, businesses, places, events and incidents are either the product of the author's imagination or used in a fictitious manner. Any resemblance to actual persons, living or dead, or actual events is purely coincidental.

Dedication

To the people of Maui

The Valley Isle

The first draft of this story was essentially finished on a Southwest flight from Phoenix to Maui in June, 2023. My wife, Jan, and I spent the week in Kaanapali with our daughter, Alycia, and her two kids (two of our grandkids)—Judah and Mathilda. Most of our time was spent on the beach, but Alycia, Judah, Mathilda and I did head into Lahaina for a few hours. The kids got Henna tattoos and we waited in line for the best Hawaii Shave Ice on the planet.

Because our son, Mike, and his wife, Amber, and our other three grandkids—Clover, Phoenix, and Decker, were not able to join us, Jan and I rescheduled their week for August 11, 2023, choosing to use it ourselves to celebrate our 44th wedding anniversary.

But, on August 8, 2023, a deadly fire roared through Lahaina, destroying that historic town, the homes and livelihood of those who lived there, and taking the lives of over 100 people.

Jan and I have had the privilege of spending time in Maui every year since 2004, with the exception of the COVID years. We've taken the road to Hana. We've ziplined. I've golfed (once). We've done whale watching. We've walked the streets of Lahaina. We have pictures of our kids from when they were little, and then of our grandkids from when they were little, in front of the Banyan tree. We've taken a walking tour of historic Lahaina. We've done a luau. We've snorkeled alongside turtles and scuba-dived at Blackrock. I long ago lost track of how many boxes of dark chocolate macadamia nuts I've gone through—which apparently originated in Maui! But most of the time, we sit on the beach and read, or listen to audiobooks and the sounds of Maui. Our favorite time of the year is whale season.

Over the course of 20 years, we have come to love the beauty of Maui and the people who live there. We are always aware that we are guests in their island home. But those one to two weeks we spend each year feel a bit like home for us, in part because of the Aloha spirit of the Islanders.

The Adventures of Toby Baxter—Book 3 finds Toby in Maui. At first I thought that, in light of the Lahaina tragedy, I should change the setting out of respect. But keeping Toby in Maui allows me to affirm my love for the Island and its people.

But I did change the title of the book shortly before publishing book 2: *RiverHome for the Holidays*. Originally, book 3 was titled: *Aloha RiverHome*. But it didn't feel right to include an excerpt in book 2 with that title months after the Lahaina fire. So I retitled the book: *The GOOD Prophecy*. Now, all these months later, I feel it's important to go back to my original title to honor Maui.

As I edit and write this dedication, I'm sitting on the deck of our room in Maui, overlooking the ocean. It's a blustery day. Lots of whitecaps on the ocean. No one on the beach. But the whales seem happy enough. And it's still Hawaii beautiful!

While our ride from the airport to our resort took us above Lahaina via the Lahaina Bypass so that we couldn't see the full impact of the fire, we did see some of it. What we did see was heartbreaking, to say the least.

While still reeling from the devastation, many in the hospitality industry thanked us for coming back. Their gratitude was heart-felt, once again demonstrating the aloha spirit of Maui. But the on-going work of rebuilding the lives of so many will go on for years.

I hope you will make a donation to the people of Maui. Here's one place you can do so: [The Hawaii Community Foundation](#).

To the people of Maui: May the Aloha spirit that you share so freely, bring hope, peace, grace, and healing to you in the years to come.

Maui Strong! Lahaina Strong!

January 27, 2024

Kaanapali, Maui, Hawaii

A Toby Baxter Primer

Toby Baxter: A 13-year-old boy from Minneapolis who is summoned to *RiverHome,* usually via his closet, by the river elves to help them in their on-going battle against the trolls. He's not big on reading books… but he does love his Marvel comic book collection. *That should count as reading, shouldn't it?*

Author: With notebook in hand, Author keeps notes on Toby's adventures, and guides him from time to time. He's writing books about Toby's Quests unbeknownst to Toby. And he likes to use big words like unbeknownst.

Thomas and Jan Baxter: Toby's parents.

Sid Douglass: Toby's school friend and occasional companion in *RiverHome.*

Rainie: The love of Toby's young life.

Derrick: The school bully and Toby's enemy.

Robin Grayson: Toby's English Lit teacher and Jan Baxter's good friend. *Inconvenient!*

The River Elves

Clovor: Commander of the River Elves.

Phoenix: Clovor's brother and collector of NFL QB's jerseys and MLB caps.

Deckor: Clovor's other brother.

Judah: Cousin to Clovor, Phoenix, and Deckor.

Mathilda: Judah's sister and a Songstress.

Donold: The Captain of the River Elf Guard.

Johanna, Victor, and Ethol: Donold's lieutenants.

The Healer

The Christmas Giant: Toby's hope and inspiration. He speaks to Toby through the voice of Toby's Grandpa Baxter. Whenever the Christmas Giant shows up, it smells like Christmas.

Drones: Large, raven-like birds. They have the ability to turn their bird heads into human heads. They serve under Donold.

The Trolls

Clygon: one-time archnemesis of Toby, baby-fied by Toby in Book 2.

Blythar: one of Clygon's minions now a part of the resistance.

Plythar: Blythar's brother and new archnemesis of Toby.

Sythar, Thytar, and Prothar: former troll servants, now adoptive parents of Clygon.

The Gnomes

Jerry.

Roxie: Jerry's daughter and Phoenix's girlfriend.

Saaba: Jerry's wolf.

Santi: Roxie's wolf.

The Ogres

Oreeo: Traitor to the ogres, now sides with Plythar.

Oreea: Oreeo's sister and captain of the ogre guard. Judah's love interest.

The Sword

Fashioned by the giants in ages past, the Sword is the life-blood of *RiverHome* and the source of Toby's power.

Loach (pronounced lay-uk; Celtic for hero). The backup sword, like a backup NFL QB, left in the care of the Baxters. Fills in if the Sword loses its power.

The Compass

On each of his adventures in *RiverHome* Toby receives a compass to guide him on his Quest and in his life.

Book 1 Compass—H.E.R.O.

Honorable: Do the right thing. Always.

Enterprising: Find your way forward.

Responsible: Use your gifts and abilities in service to others.

Original: Be yourself.

Book 2 Compass—W.I.S.E.

Wonder: Be Curious!

Insight: Be Smart!

Service: Be Kind!

Endurance: Be Resilient!

Contents

About the Author	1
Dedication	6
A Toby Baxter Primer	9
Packing	15
1. Huhū	2
2. Paradise	9
3. Haleakala	16
4. Tikvah Mountains	22
5. Bowels	30
6. P.P. Pumpernickel	37
7. Giant Hall	44
8. Story Time	54
9. Uprising	65
10. A Narrow Escape	72
11. Apparently Not Such a Narrow Escape	80
12. The Hills are Alive!	87
13. Down by the River Side	95
14. Hitting the Brakes	104
15. Para-dies	112
16. Snake Bit	123
17. Stained	132
18. Good Thinking?	138
19. Finding the G…	148
20. Finding the …OO…	156

21. Finding the… D	160
22. You Good?	168
23. Page Break	174
24. For the GOOD	179
25. A Giant Send-Off	184
26. A Lo Ha	190
27. A Nagging Feeling	195
Book 4: EyeHeart RiverHome (Excerpt)	199

Packing

"Are you finished packing yet, Toby?" yelled Mom from her bedroom.

"Yes, almost," muttered Toby Baxter. The reality was that he hadn't even started.

He dug out his duffel bag from the closet and threw in some shorts, t-shirts, a couple pairs of underwear, a pair of Thor pj's, flip-flops, swim trunks, a rash guard, and a toothbrush.

"Don't forget to pack *Of Mice and Men*. Robin… er… Mrs Grayson said you're to read the first three chapters on vacation."

"I'm not bringing a stupid book on vacation," Toby said a bit too loudly.

"What's that, dear?"

"I can't wait to read it, Mom," he shouted back.

"That's what I thought you said."

He threw the book into his backpack. At least the title sounded interesting. Maybe it was a Stephen King-type horror story about rogue mice invading a small town.

"And remember to bring a sweat shirt, some warm gloves, and a stocking cap," mom shouted.

For Hawaii?

In addition to *Of Mice and Men,* he filled up his backpack with the important stuff—iPad, headphones, *Marvel* comic books, and a few candy bars.

He'd had to rummage through his closet to find his headphones buried under clothes that hadn't seen the light of day for months, or a washing-machine for that matter. Who knew what kinds of gross stuff grew in the dirty clothes of young thirteen-year-old boys.

What he didn't notice, through all of the digging in his closet, was a leather bag hidden in the back corner. And, as he shut the closet door, the faint glow seeping through the small opening of the bag…

1. Huhū

Toby Baxter was in a foul mood. And foul was a good word for it. He'd been like this for months, and not sure why. Everything and everyone seemed to rub him the wrong way. He'd had some massive explosions with his parents lately, and that had never happened before. In the moment, it seemed justified. Parents could be so *irritating!* Later on, he'd feel sick about it. Only to get into another heated argument over silly stuff. All he wanted to do was to hibernate in his room and hide himself away in his *Marvel* comic books.

Even Sid, his best friend, had noticed. Thankfully, Sid was a good friend who put up with Toby's bouts of moodiness. But he could tell that even Sid was starting to get miffed with him. *Miffed? Even these words are getting irritating.*

He had no idea what the deal was. Whatever it was, it hit him almost overnight. Most of the time, he was angry. Sometimes, in the quiet of his room, he would tear up, overwhelmed with sadness. Then, moments of surprising happiness. His mood seemed to change quickly and with little reason.

His parents had insisted that he talk things over with a counselor. After a few sessions, the therapist assured Toby and his parents that he was not depressed. Moodiness, the therapist explained, can be normal for teenagers, even for teenage boys. Apparently, one of the toughest periods in a human being's development is middle-school boyhood. *Who'd have thought?* Toby had thought. The therapist recommended that Toby continue to meet with him once a month, be patient, and stay connected to his parents, his friends, and his church. The moodiness would pass. Eventually.

That was three weeks ago. And he was still in the grip of it on and off.

And now, he was stuck in the middle seat on a jet about to fly from Minneapolis to Honolulu and then on to Maui. He'd lost a two-out-of-three rock, paper, scissors competition to Sid for the aisle seat. The big man in the window seat on the other side of Toby forced him to have to lean a bit toward Sid. It would be like this for hours!

He was hoping that, once he stepped off of the plane in Maui, his mood would change. He'd been looking forward to this since his parents surprised him with the trip on Christmas, saying that Sid could join them. They'd worked it out with Sid's mom, who was still a bit skittish after Sid's Christmas break adventure at the Baxter house—or, more specifically, on the other side of Toby's closet. It took forever for spring break to finally come. But it did, and now Toby was sardined in the middle seat. That's how he had gone from a bad mood to a foul mood.

Aloha!

The word had been whispered into his left ear. He turned to look at the man in the window seat. The man flashed him a big, warm smile. Toby had seen it before. The Christmas Giant! For a moment, the thought of him, and the brief smell of Christmas cookies, filled him with hope.

He rubbed his eyes and looked back at the man. But the man's head was buried in his phone, oblivious to Toby, looking nothing like his big friend.

The flight attendants were explaining how to buckle a seat belt. Toby ignored them and began digging into his backpack, looking for his headphones and iPad.

Sid nudged him and said, "I think that flight attendant is trying to get your attention."

Toby looked up and saw... *Author?*

Author was wearing a bright orange Hawaiian shirt with some sort of flower pattern on it, cargo shorts, flip-flops, and a lei over his shoulders. His dark bald head shined like a bowling ball. Because of his height, it kept hitting the ceiling of the plane.

Toby noticed a pencil parked behind his left ear.

...in the case of the loss of cabin pressure, oxygen masks will fall from above. Simply put the mask over your head and cover your mouth...

Author demonstrated the proper use of the oxygen mask and then proceeded to put on a yellow water vest...

... in the unlikely event of a water landing...

Toby looked around to see if anyone else saw the words in the small space above Author's head. But nobody seemed to be paying attention to him.

It appears that you have been having some rough days, Toby.

Toby looked around again, this time to see if anyone was looking at him. But now, everyone was frozen in time.

"How did you know, and what are you doing here?"

I wanted to give you something that will, hopefully, lift your spirits and get you back to being Toby Baxter.

"I think I've forgotten who he is, to be honest. I've been in a pretty angry mood lately," Toby said.

Since you're headed to Hawaii, the Hawaiian word for anger is huhū. But let's see if we can turn that huhū to hauʻoli.

"Which means…?"

Joy!

"I'd settle for less moody…"

What you need is a good story. Something that will fill your dendrites and nephrons with positive energy…

"My what and what?"

Look in your backpack.

"I was just doing that, trying to find my…"

Toby dug deeper into his backpack but couldn't find his headphones or his iPad. Instead, he found a leather bag.

"How did that get here?"

Do you remember walking out of the bathroom before you boarded?

"Yes, I do! Some idiot…"

Language!

"Sorry. Some guy, not paying attention, ran right into me, sending my backpack sprawling onto the concourse floor, along with all of the contents, as I was in the process of zipping it shut. Admittedly, he was extremely sorry and helped me repack it. What about it?"

Picture the man in your mind, Toby. Take a deep breath, close your eyes, and see his face…

Toby closed his eyes. He took two deep breaths. And he concentrated not on the stuff that had spilled onto the floor but on the face of the man… *wait… not a man… a … no!… how did I miss it…*

"Phoenix? It was Phoenix? How did I miss seeing that it was him?"

You didn't notice him because you were so upset about your backpack spilling onto the floor. And I think Phoenix was in a bit of a hurry. He wanted to grab a few Minnesota Vikings jerseys before heading back to *RiverHome*. Things are not, shall we say, in a good way.

"Is *RiverHome* in danger? Is Clygon back at it again? But he's still a baby, isn't he? What's going on, Author? Is that what this bag is for?"

"Look inside."

Toby subconsciously noted that the words were no longer above Author's head, meaning he was into a new story. But his attention was on the leather bag. He opened it and, to his surprise, found the fragments of the Sword, broken and shattered somehow by Clygon. The fragments began to glow.

"I don't understand. Why did Phoenix give me this?"

"It's been in your closet since the moment you came back from *RiverHome* last Christmas. Deckor put it there for safe-keeping. But now you need to get it back to *RiverHome*. The river elves and their allies are vulnerable with the Sword incapacitated."

"Inca-what?"

"Incapacitated—deprived of its power. *Loach* is weakening. It was never meant to carry the full power of the Sword. Because of it, *RiverHome* is in grave danger—or serious doo-doo, as you kids like to say."

"Ah... actually we don't. And from who?"

"Whom."

"Whom what?"

"Plythar. He's ashamed at the loss of power the trolls suffered after you baby-fied Clygon. He's assembled an army of trolls bent on breaking the new alliance between the river elves, the gnomes, the ogres, and the trolls who had once sided with Clygon. And with *Loach* losing strength, his growing power is putting *RiverHome* at risk."

"But what can I do about it? Obviously, I'm on this plane, and we're headed to Hawaii. How am I supposed to do anything? And what am I supposed to do with this?" he asked, holding up the leather bag. "I left my closet back at the house, so I have no way into *RiverHome.*"

Author laughed. "That was actually quite clever, Toby. I'm going to need to write that one down. But not to worry. *RiverHome* will find you. Once it does, you will need to find the giants, so that they can remake the Sword."

"But the giants don't exist anymore, do they?"

Author rubbed his chin and smiled.

Toby felt the jet lurch as it began to move back from the gate.

"Finally!" Sid said. "Hawaii, here we come!"

Toby looked up, and Author was gone.

2. Paradise

It had been 59 degrees and cloudy when they left Minneapolis. Now, on the Kaanapali beach, 79 sunny degrees and humid. Paradise after a long, cold winter.

The rooms were ready when they arrived at the *Westin*. Toby and Sid had their own room! They quickly threw on their trunks, flip-flops and some reef-safe sunscreen and headed into the ocean. Hawaii was four hours behind Minneapolis, so they had an hour before dinner to swim. The water was crystal clear and warm. Tomorrow they would rent snorkel gear so they could explore the reefs and the ocean life. Hopefully they would see a turtle or two.

After a quick shower, they walked over to *Whalers Village* with Thomas and Jan Baxter, Toby's parents, to find something to eat. Toby suggested *Haagen Das,* but Mom said they needed to eat real food first. The little food court on the lower level proved the best bet with a few options—the top choice being pizza. And then *Haagen Das*—specifically two scoops of chocolate ice cream topped with hot cocoa fudge and chocolate chips. Toby's mom opted for the *Ono Gelato* store.

They made a brief stop at the *ABC Store* to get some water and juice for the morning, then walked along the beach down to the *Sheraton Hotel* and took in the sunset. They watched as one of the torch lighters climbed up Black Rock, lighting torches along the way, and then dived into the ocean. Once in a while, Toby would see a spout of water shimmering in the sunlight, alerting him to a nearby whale. But no breaches so far…

And then… there it was, within eyesight. A huge whale jumped up out of the water, landing with a splash that could be heard on the beach. The whole crowd involuntarily cheered and applauded.

"Do it again!" Sid shouted.

And, as if on cue, the whale offered an encore.

A great start to a great vacation. Toby's foul mood had vanished, for now. He was feeling much more himself.

By 8 pm, they were exhausted, as it was midnight Minneapolis time. Their third-floor room overlooked the pools. They would try the pool slide tomorrow before snorkeling. But for now, with the patio door open, allowing in the sound of the crashing waves, Toby and Sid fell asleep.

But not before Sid said, "Toby, could you turn that flashlight in your backpack off?"

Toby heard what sounded like pieces of metal hitting each other. He had been in a deep sleep and was working hard to open his eyes. As he did, a bright light blinded him. He could hear Sid snoring gently from the other bed, almost in rhythm with the crashing of the ocean waves.

He looked toward the source of the light, which was coming from the floor. He could make out what appeared to be a person, crouched over the light, but had no idea who or what it was.

Toby sat up, drawing the attention of the person on the floor.

"Ah, Toby," the voice said. "So sorry to wake you."

It was Clovor, his river elf friend.

"What are you doing here?" Toby asked. "And what are you doing there?"

As his eyes adjusted, he saw that she was trying to jigsaw the Sword back together.

Clovor stood up and sat next to him on the bed. She had cut her hair since the last time he saw her. No longer hanging over her shoulders, her hair, with a streak of purple, was now cropped at the bottom of her neck, and shorter on the sides, accenting her pointy ears. Her bangs were shorter as well, highlighting her Mr Spock eye brows. She looked much healthier, too, since the last time he had seen her. She wore leather pants and a T-shirt that read, *Phoenix went to Minneapolis and all he got me was this silly T-shirt*. Off to the side, he saw her quiver, holding several arrows.

She noticed that he noticed the quiver and said, "Can't be too careful."

After a few moments, he re-asked his questions, "What are you doing here, and what were you doing there?" nodding toward the floor.

"The sword *Loach* is weakening." She pronounced it *lay-uk*, the Celtic word for hero. *Loach* served as a backup to the Sword. Toby had planted it in the Sword's monument in *RiverHome* on his last trip over there. "I think Plythar is gaining strength. We need the Sword repaired. I'm here to make sure all of the pieces of the Sword are accounted for. It's going to take a miracle to put it back together. In fact, we have no idea how to do it. The giants who created the Sword, as you know, are gone… or at least we think they're gone… or if they're not gone, we don't know how to find them. But if even one piece is missing, then not even a miracle can help us."

"And…"

"All the pieces seem to be here. So now we're down to a miracle."

"And…"

"And what?"

"Now that you know you have all of the pieces, what's next? Are you taking the Sword back to *RiverHome?*" Toby asked.

Clovor started to speak, then stopped and tipped her head as if listening to something.

"Pack up the Sword and hide it in your closet. Pretend you're asleep. I'll distract them and lead them away from you!"

"Distract who?"

"No questions, Toby. Do as I say. Now!"

Toby quickly packed up the Sword and, after a moment or two of hesitation, stuffed it into the safe in the closet. He set the four-number password using the day and month of his birth as the code, locked it, shut the closet door, and jumped into bed.

His room door slowly opened. Then quietly closed. He knew at once from the smell of sweat and vomit that the intruder was a troll. He put a pillow over his head and pretended to be asleep.

"Go no further, or this arrow will find itself in your eye," Clovor snarled.

"Not through these industrial strength goggles I grabbed from the maintenance room downstairs it won't," growled the troll. "You can't be too prepared, as Plythar says. Especially when taking on an arrow-slinging river rat."

"I'm assuming you're looking for this?"

Toby took a peek to see Clovor holding up a bag, hoping the troll would mistake it for the Sword bag.

"I am. And if you let me have it now, no harm will come to that coward pretending to be asleep under his pillow. We always knew Toby Baxter was a fake."

Toby wasn't about to argue. He'd felt the same way both times in *RiverHome,* no matter what his friends had said.

"I'm afraid you've got me, troll! Toby, could you do us a favor?"

Toby slowly pulled the pillow off of his head and climbed out of bed. The moonlight shining through the windows helped him see the outline of the troll.

"Could you hand this bag to our new friend?"

"What? You want to surrender the Sword?" Toby asked, acting on a hunch that Clovor had a plan.

"It's you or the Sword, Toby, and you will always be more important to me than any sword!"

Toby took the bag and slowly walked it over to the troll. As he handed it over, he heard a zing, and instantly, an arrow embedded itself in the troll's chest, expertly placed in a small seam in his armor, knocking him onto the floor.

"Quickly, Toby. I've been careless. He must have followed me here. Help me drag him to the closet."

"What? You're going to leave a dead troll in my closet? How am I supposed to explain that to housekeeping? And the smell is killing me."

"Of course, I'm not asking you to keep him. I'm taking him with me. And he's not dead. Only wounded. Hopefully he can provide some information for us on what Plythar is up to."

"But why the closet? Is the portal there?"

"Yes, but I can only use it this once, so no, to answer the question you're going to ask, you can't come with me."

They dragged the troll across the floor to the small closet. When Toby opened the closet door, he was met with a mist from the waterfall on the other side of the closet wall.

Clovor stepped in, grabbed the troll by the shoulders and began to drag him into the closet.

"What about the Sword?" Toby asked.

"Keep it safe until…"

And with that, Clovor and the troll were gone, and the closet wall reappeared. Toby reached in to tap on it. No doubt about it. It was a closet wall.

"It stinks in here," Sid said sleepily. "Next time go easy on the pizza!"

3. Haleakala

The knock on the door was quiet at first, and then grew more urgent. Toby had just fallen back to sleep. He rolled over and looked at the clock. *2:00 am! Who in the world?*

"Toby..." The whisper came from the other side of the door. "We have a surprise for you." It was his dad. "Open the door."

Toby sleepily opened the door and let his dad in. Sid, hearing the noise, sat up, scratched his head, got up, and headed to the bathroom.

"It smells awful in here!" Toby's dad said. "It smells like... like..." His eyes widened.

"Don't ask," Toby said. "Clovor took care of it."

"Care of what?" Sid asked, wiping his hands on his pajamas.

"Why are you waking us up at 2 in the morning?" Toby asked his dad.

"We have a surprise for you. We're going on a bike trip."

"Now? At 2:00 am?"

"The shuttle will be here in 30 minutes. We're biking down Haleakala, a volcano, and we need to get there for sunrise. It will start out cold, so cram a few layers into your backpacks..."

"So that's why mom told me to bring a sweatshirt and a stocking cap…"

"… and meet us in the lobby by 2:30."

"Mom is going, too?"

"She wouldn't miss it. It's apparently one of the best things to do in Maui."

As dad walked out the door, Toby and Sid quickly got dressed and loaded up their backpacks.

"Did I hear you mention Clovor? Was she here? Does that vile smell mean we had a troll in the room?" Sid tried to act nonchalant— *or is it nonchalantly?*—but Toby could hear the excitement in his voice.

"It was something to do with the Sword locked away in the safe."

"Wait… What? The Sword is in our room?"

"I'll fill you in later. Not much to tell, really. But it's 2:25, and we need to get downstairs."

In addition to Toby's parents, another couple waited in the lobby, apparently a part of their group. The van arrived at 2:30 on the dot. *What does 'on the dot' even mean?* The driver told them that they had two other hotel stops before they headed up the volcano. Toby fell asleep before the van pulled out of the *Westin* driveway and didn't wake up until they were at the top of the mountain ninety minutes later.

It was still dark, but Toby thought he could see the faint outline of light breaking in. The tour guide explained that the ride was 24 miles downhill. They would stop at various points along the volcano road to enjoy the views and learn some history. Toby was grateful his mom had told him to pack warm clothes because it was cold! The guide assured them they'd heat up soon enough.

They'd be riding mountain bikes equipped with special brakes that could handle the steep 6500-foot drop from start to finish. It had a much different feel from his bike at home, but Toby could tell that this was going to be epic.

Toby's mom walked over and hugged him, and then Sid. "I'm kind of nervous," she whispered to the two of them. "It's been a while since I've ridden a bike. The last time was years ago. Mr B and I were on a group bike ride in Washington D.C. at the end of a week-long bike trip that started in Gettysburg. Unfortunately, I misjudged the space between two metal pylons right in front of the Lincoln Memorial. I crashed and badly bruised my ribs. It was a long flight home that afternoon! So you boys keep me safe, okay?"

They climbed onto their bikes. The sun was just starting to peek out on the horizon.

"Let's go!" the tour guide yelled. Slowly, one by one, they lifted their feet off of the ground, placed them on the pedals, and started to coast down the volcano into the sunrise.

Toby couldn't believe how peaceful it was. And how breathtaking. As he looked to his right, he noticed that they were actually above the clouds, the sun turning them a bright orange.

This would be a good time to practice some vocabulary words... He could hear Mrs Grayson's voice in his head...

Exhilarating… Invigorating… Stimulating… Wow! I really do need a vacation from school.

Sid, being Sid, was woo-hooing and laughing and woo-hooing some more. Toby quickly looked back to see that Mom had a big smile on her face, but he could tell that her hands were millimeters away from the brakes. Dad rode up to Toby and gave him a thumbs up before slowing down to get back in line behind Mom.

The sun was slowly rising as they quickly flew down the hill. Up ahead… *can you go up ahead when you're going down a hill?*… Toby could see a low-hanging cloud covering the road in front of them. *This was going to be cool! Riding into a cloud!*

Sid was the first into it, still woo-hooing, followed by Toby.

Toby instantly felt the cool mist from the cloud on his face. It stung a bit because of the cold. He found it hard to see through the fog, so he slowed down, hoping Mom and Dad did the same. He could no longer hear Sid woo-hooing and wondered if the cloud muted sounds. It seemed to be taking a long time to get to the other side of it.

He experienced a tinge of fear. Something didn't feel right. It had grown dark. In fact, too dark. It created the sense that he wasn't moving.

Then he realized that he wasn't moving. He was no longer on his bike. He was standing in complete darkness. A darkness so dark that he couldn't see his hand in front of his face. And the silence was deafening. *Is that an oxymoron?* All he could hear was his breathing.

He stood still. He tried to calm himself. He reached out his hands. Nothing in front of him. He reached out to his sides. Still nothing. He reached up and stood on his toes. Still nothing.

He slowly moved to his left, his armed raised. It took him several steps, but he finally felt something solid. He took off his gloves and felt a rough rock wall. He moved several steps to his right and felt the same thing.

He was in a cave.

What am I doing in a cave?

He began to panic. He could feel the walls closing in on him, making him feel claustrophobic. He was about to scream…

…when he saw two green eyes coming toward him.

He held his breath. He closed his eyes… *like that's going to make me invisible.* He could hear whatever it was getting closer and closer…

… and then he felt a big slurpy lick across his face.

He recognized that lick. It was Saaba, Jerry the Gnome's faithful wolf!

What is he doing here?

Toby leaned down, reaching out his arms. Saaba snuggled up to him, and Toby buried his head into the wolf, releasing his panic through his tears. But the tears didn't last long. He heard another noise. He looked up and saw a light coming toward him. He heard a voice call out: "Saaba?"

Shivers raced up and down Toby's back. He knew that voice. It sounded younger. But there was no mistaking it.

Clygon!

4. Tikvah Mountains

The light drew closer, creating weird shadows on the walls. Toby couldn't quite make out its source. It wasn't a torch. More like an orb in a holder radiating blue energy. Something out of *The Rings of Power* on *Amazon Prime*.

Eventually, Toby could see the outline of Clygon. He was about Toby's height, but much bigger, as in ripped! His face was the face Toby remembered, but much younger, with the typically large troll nose, minus the huge wart that had been there the last time Toby had seen him. He still had oversized ears. His troll hair had changed dramatically, no longer looking like straw poking out all over the place. He seemed... *groomed?* He was wearing leathers—the kind the river elves wore. *How was that possible?* And the smell of sweat and vomit didn't waft over him. *Waft?*

The last time he had seen Clygon, Clygon was an infant. Through the singing of Christmas carols, the adult Clygon had grown backward. He now looked to be about Toby's age.

"Don't come any closer," Toby said, trying to sound like he was in control.

Clygon stopped. Then he smiled. That smile had played havoc with Toby's intestines in the past. But this time, the smile seemed genuine.

The two of them stood staring at each other.

Toby was the first one to break.

"What are you doing here?"

"I'm here to find you, of course."

Toby felt another shiver of fear.

"Why?"

Clygon didn't answer for a moment.

"I get that you don't trust me."

"Of course I don't trust you. You tried to kill me. Twice!"

"True. Sorry about that."

Another staring contest.

"A mutual friend sent me, Toby. He said that you should look into your heart."

"What's that supposed to—" Toby stopped. He heard a quiet whisper.

Trust him.

It was the Christmas Giant. The voice of his Grandpa Baxter. Toby could faintly smell peppermint hot chocolate.

"Have you seen him?" Toby asked.

Clygon's face suddenly clouded over.

Wow! Toby thought. *I'd heard that phrase used before and thought it was a metaphor. Or a hypothesis. Or an alliteration. Or whatever. But a literal cloud just moved across his face.*

Behind the cloud was a frown.

"No," Clygon answered him. "No one has seen him since… since… I…"

"Since you murdered him!"

Clygon took a step back at the force of Toby's anger. The shock on Clygon's face blew up the cloud.

"No!" Clygon pleaded. "It wasn't like that…"

"It wasn't like what? He was dead when Clovor and I were marched into that hall."

"No. Yes. He was dead. But I didn't kill him. We didn't kill him. We brought him into the hall so he could see me defeat you. I believed that he was the power behind your power… the power behind the Sword. To defeat you would defeat him, so I thought. When he arrived, he was… um … he didn't look well. He seemed weak. That's why he was sitting on the ground, leaning against the wall. He had no strength. And then… he… it was like he'd run out of breath. He was gone."

Toby found himself back in the prison cell in *Ogreton Heights,* along with Clovor and the Christmas Giant. He watched as the guards came for the Giant; how the Giant leaned down and breathed onto him and Clovor. He remembered the moment when both he and Clovor felt the Giant die, only to have that feeling confirmed by the ringing of bells celebrating his death. He could still picture walking into the grand hall in *Ogreton Heights* to face Clygon, seeing the slumped, lifeless body of the Giant off to the side.

And he remembered something else.

"I saw him, you know."

Clygon's mouth dropped. Not onto the floor or anything like that. But it definitely opened in surprise.

"You saw him? After he died?"

"He looked different, but it was definitely the Christmas Giant. He... he... well... he glowed. Like a spirit. But I was pretty sure if I had the chance, I could hug him."

Clygon stood still for a long moment. And then his face brightened. Almost literally. A smile had replaced the shock.

"I've not seen him, Toby. I only hear his whisper. Like you did just now. He told me... he said he was giving me a do-over!" Clygon sighed. "You can smell the Christmas cookies, right?" he asked.

"Actually, I smell peppermint hot chocolate."

Clygon nodded.

"Well... if that's not enough to convince you, then ask Saaba."

"Saaba can't talk."

"Saaba!" Clygon said. "Here, boy."

Saaba jumped up, ran over to Clygon, threw his paws onto Clygon's shoulders, and planted a wet, sloppy kiss on him.

"Still not convinced? Then look at this."

Clygon held out his right hand. "May I come closer?"

Without waiting for an answer, Clygon lowered the bright orb and showed Toby the top of his right hand, bearing the green mark of the river elves from his wrist to his middle knuckle. It was the same mark Toby had received on his first visit to *RiverHome*.

"Clovor marked me just before I headed here."

"You've joined the river elves?" Toby's head was spinning.

"Hold steady, Toby. Yes. Look. Your Christmas Carol sing-along gave me the opportunity to start over. The Christmas Giant thankfully gave me a second chance. And my new parents, Prothar, Sythar, and Thytar, ended up raising me in *RiverHome* to protect me from Plythar."

Clygon held out his hand one more time. Toby tentatively reached for it. The two of them shook hands. Clygon's hand felt like sandpaper.

Toby over-relaxed. He'd been so tense that once he let go of the stress, he fell to the ground.

Saaba rushed to him, as did Clygon.

"Here. Take a few sips of this. You may recognize it."

Toby took a long sip of the familiar *RiverHome* drink. It filled him with energy and heightened his senses.

Clygon sat next to him.

"How did you know I'd be here?" Toby asked and then answered his own question: "The Christmas Giant."

Clygon nodded.

"And where are we?"

"We, my new friend, are in the bowels of the Tikvah Mountains."

From Hawaii to bowels... Toby muttered.

"Tikvah Mountains... Isn't this the home of the..."

"That's right. The giants," Clygon answered.

"But... they don't exist anymore, do they?"

"Well..." Clygon let the thought hang in the dark air.

"Well, what?"

"Perhaps we should start with a different question. Why are you here?"

"Okay, why am I here?"

"Because we need to get the Sword repaired and back to *RiverHome*."

"Two problems," Toby said. "One... The Sword is in Maui..."

"Look in your backpack."

"Huh?"

Toby pulled off his backpack. As he did so, he saw light glowing from it—The Sword!

"How did that… get there? I left it locked up in the safe in my room."

"Mathilda snuck into your room and put it in your backpack. You really shouldn't be leaving the Sword where any troll can steal it."

Toby ignored the rebuke and, at the same time, wondered how Mathilda had figured out the code to the safe.

"Problem number two… only the giants can fix it. And the giants no longer exist…"

"Is that true, Toby? Do they no longer exist? Or is it just that no one has seen or heard from them for a long time? Maybe they've gone underground… literally."

"So the giants still exist? And they're in these mountains? How do you know?"

Again, Toby answered his own question.

"The Christmas Giant. So… where are they?"

"That, Toby, is a good question. No one knows. But we need to find them, if indeed they do exist, as soon as possible."

"And how are we supposed to do that?"

"Another good question. I have no idea. Yet. Our friend CG…"

"CG?"

"Christmas Giant… said we'll discover the answer once we set out on the Quest."

"Quest?"

"To find the giants and defeat Plythar, of course."

Clygon stood up. He offered his hand to Toby and helped him up.

"Here. The river elves sent this for you. This backpack has some of the essentials you'll need for our adventure, including a change of clothes, a sleeping bag and pillow, some hand wipes, a shovel…"

"Speaking of shovels… and bowels… um… in the woods… on the way to your stronghold… I was able to… ah… um… you know, dig a hole… when I… um needed to…"

Clygon started to laugh. "Go on, Toby. Finish your thought."

Toby was sure he was blushing.

"Obviously I can't dig a hole in the rock…"

"Follow me. I found a spot earlier that should work. Heel, Saaba."

Clygon headed down into the cave, followed by Saaba. Toby could hear Clygon's laugh bouncing off the walls.

"Imagine Saaba, Toby Baxter and I on a Quest together to save *RiverHome!*"

That… Toby thought… *is an interesting plot twist.*

5. Bowels

After a short walk, they stopped. Clygon pointed with his fire orb to a spot that looked like a stone bench. Behind it, a drop of several feet. And wafting... *again with the wafting?*... up from it was that noxious smell of troll poop.

"You've already been here by the smell of it," Toby gagged out.

"I told you I'd found a spot earlier. Do your business and do it quickly. Something doesn't feel quite right."

Great. That will help speed things up.

The stone was cold to the touch, but it served its purpose. The wipes proved to be essential, as they had on his previous visits to *RiverHome*, for several reasons.

Toby moved away from the make-shift latrine and its toxic fumes and huddled up with Clygon and Saaba.

"What doesn't feel right?" Toby said while chewing on a piece of beef jerky he'd grabbed from his new backpack. He'd transferred the Sword to it and left his Hawaii backpack behind. It would be too much to carry.

"Saaba sensed it first. Nothing concrete, I'm afraid. Just a feeling at this point. So let's get moving."

"Get moving where?"

"Down into the bowels of Tikvah. That's the best I can do for now. By the way, you'll need this."

Clygon handed Toby an orb torch thingy. Clygon said a few words over it that Toby didn't understand, and it began to glow.

"What is this, and how did you do that, and can I do it?"

"It's something the river elves have been working on for years and finally perfected. It's called an *Elf Orb*. It's made of a liquid substance of some sort that they found by accident in one of the river elf homes. Their hills are filled with the stuff, and they had no idea. The orb itself is made of crystal."

"What did you say over it to make it light up?"

Clygon laughed. "I did that for dramatic effect. All you have to do is shake it, and it lights up for hours."

Toby took hold of it. It was much lighter than he expected... *did I just step into a homonym? Not for the first time in RiverHome.*

Saaba took the lead and they started once again moving down into the mountain. Because the walkways were carved out for giants, Toby didn't experience the claustrophobia close spaces normally caused. And the air movement kept things fresh and cool.

They had to move cautiously so as not to trip. After about thirty minutes—though it was hard to tell how much time had passed in the darkness—the walk became monotonous. The darkness started to get to him.

He'd not been paying attention and walked into Clygon. And it hurt. *That guy is like a rock wall himself! Was that a simile or a metaphor?*

Clygon turned to him with a finger to his lips. His eyes wide.

Saaba growled.

They heard high-pitched screeching. More like the combination of thousands of tiny screeches. The kind that gets into your bowels and turns them to mush.

The screeching was followed by what sounded like a windstorm headed straight at them.

Suddenly, tiny, beady eyes surrounded them. Toby could feel something like gnats swarming around his face. But the swarming felt like little pin-pricks.

"Try not to move," Clygon whispered. "Shake your *Elf Orb* to douse the light. It's the light that attracts them. And cover your face!"

The cave was now pitcher than pitch dark with the exception of the tiny eyes. Loud buzzing—the sound of zillions of mosquitoes—moved past them, but not before hundreds more pin-pricks to the face, which Toby did his best to cover.

They didn't move for several minutes to make sure that whatever those things were were gone.

Toby saw Clygon's *Elf Orb* spring back to life, so he shook his on as well. He could see little specks of blood on Clygon's face and suspected his face bore the same marks.

"Stalagmites..." Clygon muttered.

"Stalagmites? Aren't those the long tubes that grow on a cave floor?"

"What? No! Stalagmites are tiny mites that feed off of flesh, any kind of flesh. They make quick jabs into the skin with micro-needles sticking out of their tails, drawing a micro-amount of blood. Think of mosquitoes on steroids. But get attacked by too many of them, and the poison they leave behind can make you very, very sick."

Toby was already feeling ill.

"What are the symptoms?"

"Numbness... followed by vertigo... followed by severe swelling... followed by the inability to swallow..."

"I think I have all of those!" Toby said.

Clygon held the orb up to Toby's face.

"Nah, you'll be fine. Besides, we have the antidote. The river elf drink works wonders for stalagmite bites. Have a sip just to be on the safe side. And use a hand wipe to wash off your face. It has antibacterial properties."

The wipe stung, but his face started to feel better almost immediately, although it also felt fat and swollen.

"If you have stalagmites, do you also have stalactites?"

"You don't want to know."

"Great!"

Saaba turned, and they followed him down deeper into the cave. Toby could feel the pressure in his ears. Occasionally, he would pinch his nose and blow, clearing his head. He wasn't sure if that was a good idea or not, but it helped. The air seemed to get more stale...

or is it staler?... the deeper they went, making it harder to get deep breaths.

Clygon eventually called a halt to their walk, much to Toby's appreciation. His feet, having walked on the uneven stone for hours, were sore, as were his legs, his back, and his face, still hurting from the stalagmites.

Clygon took a moment or two to shine his light orb around.

"This looks like as good a place as any to settle in for the night."

"How are we supposed to sleep on this hard rock?" Toby asked, looking around for a soft spot to land.

"On this."

Clygon reached into his backpack and pulled out what looked like a thin sheet.

"How's that supposed to help?" asked Toby.

"Watch!"

Clygon took the sheet by its edges and shook it out. As if by magic it morphed into a sleeping bag—a plush, comfortable sleeping bag.

Toby reached into his backpack and found his own magical sleeping bag. To his surprise, on top of the surprise of the sleeping bag itself, he found a nice, firm but comfortable pillow.

He and Clygon ate a simple meal of jerky and washed it down with the river elf drink. They then took turns at a new make-shift latrine.

Toby tucked into his sleeping bag and punched his pillow a few times to get it just right.

"How lost are we?" he asked Clygon.

Clygon laughed.

"I have no idea where we are, Toby. But not to worry. Saaba has a nose for finding what we're looking for."

Saaba curled up next to Toby. He'd missed the comfort of the wolf next to him as he slept. But not so much the big, sloppy good-night kiss.

Not only was it pitch dark in the cave, it was also pitch silent. All he could hear was the gentle hum of Saaba's breathing and the light snoring of Clygon. He'd been able to sleep through Sid's snoring, so Clygon's shouldn't prove to be a problem.

He was in that middle space, in between sleep and awakeness. *Is awakeness a word?* He heard laughter. Coming from deep somewhere. It could be a dream. He hoped it was a dream. But the laughter grew closer. As did the sound of loud footsteps.

He opened his eyes… or maybe he dreamed he was opening his eyes. No. He was opening his eyes because Saaba was on the alert next to him, a low growl building in his chest. He could feel Clygon sitting up, grabbing a sword.

Then… a bright light. A gigantic foot landed inches from his head. A booming laugh.

"Well… well… well…" a big voice said. "Who do we have here? A wolf. A troll. And a human. Is that you, Toby Baxter? We've been waiting for you… for a very long time."

6. P.P. Pumpernickel

Toby's eyes had a hard time adjusting to the light. Apparently, whoever was holding it noticed and turned it down. Toby sat up and looked up. In front of him stood...

"Are you a giant?" Toby asked.

"Toby! We found them! We found them! We found the giants!" Clygon couldn't contain his laughter. "We found them!" He was jumping up and down.

The giant in front of them let out a big booming laugh of his own.

"I think it's more like we found you."

It was a deep male voice attached to a body about nine feet tall. He wore hiking boots, jeans, and a red-plaided flannel shirt with elbow patches on the elbows... *where else would the elbow patches be? His stubble-covered face held a large nose—of course it would. He was a giant after all*—big ears, and translucent eyes—the kind of eyes that have been in the dark a long, long time. The sides of his head were shaved, and the top of his head sported a patch of purple hair. *Purple hair?*

The giant reached down his massive hand and helped Toby to his feet. It looked like the hand of an adult reaching out to the hand of a toddler. Toby, at almost six feet, came up to the giant's chest. Clygon jumped up next to him.

"You must be Clygon," the giant rumbled. "We've had our eyes on you, young troll. So good to see the new you."

Clygon seemed embarrassed.

Toby couldn't take his eyes off of the purple hair, and the giant noticed.

"I found a bottle of my daughter's purple dye on our kitchen counter. In a moment of foolishness, I decided to try to put a streak of it in my hair, but I muffed it up. My wife had to dye all of my hair!"

He laughed a big, jolly laugh.

"I'm still trying to get used to it. My wife loves it, but my kids think I'm a bit old for it. They think I'm trying too hard to be hip."

Hip? Sounds like something Author would say. He must be old like Author. A boomer, perhaps?

"You said you had been waiting for me. What did you mean by that? And where have you been? Everyone thought you had disappeared. And how did you know we would be here? Even I didn't know we were here until a few hours ago." The questions poured out of Toby.

The giant laughed his big, booming laugh.

"All in good time, Toby Baxter. Courtesy says I should introduce myself first. I'm P.P. Pumpernickel."

He bowed slightly to them.

"P.P. Pumpernickel?" Clygon asked with awe. "As in *the* P.P. Pumpernickel? Of the ancient Pumpernickel giants? Of the Sword-making Pumpernickels?"

"The same," P.P. Pumpernickel bowed slightly once again.

"But… but… you must be…" Clygon began

"Old? Ancient?" laughed P.P. Pumpernickel. "We giants live for centuries, as you know, young Clygon. I have seen many, many stories in my life so far."

"What does P.P. stand for?" Toby asked, breaking the momentary silence as Clygon tried to process the giant standing before them.

"The first P is for Peter. The second P is for Peter."

"Wait. So you're Peter Peter Pumpernickel? As in, Peter Peter Pumpernickel, had a wife and couldn't keep her?"

"Close, but not quite," Pumpernickel laughed. "That's Peter Peter Pumpkin Eater, of a different story."

"Oh. Right. Sorry. But why Peter Peter?"

"My father's father's name is Peter, and my mother's father's name is Peter. So, I'm named after my grandfathers, obviously.

Toby's head was spinning.

"It's a giant thing. To make things easy, just call me Pumpernickel."

"Are your parents still alive?"

"They are. As are my grandparents and great grandparents."

"So if you're ancient, they must be…"

"As old as the earth, Toby Baxter."

"Wow!" Toby and Clygon both said together, with an assist from Saaba.

"We have a lot to talk about. But you must both be tired. Our home is not far from here. We have food. Soft beds. And very nice WCs."

"WCs?" Toby whispered to Clygon.

"It stands for Water Closets."

"Water Closets?"

"Toilets!"

"Fantastic!" Toby said a bit too enthusiastically. He was tired of sitting on hard rock walls. "Just the ticket!" *Just the ticket?*

Pumpernickel turned and then stopped.

"You do have the Sword, Toby Baxter?"

Toby pointed to his backpack.

"Good!"

Pumpernickel turned again and then stopped again.

"Forgive me. I have forgotten my manners. Let me introduce you to two of our junior leaders."

Two giants stepped out from the shadows. A male and female.

"This is Oliver, my younger brother."

Oliver bowed.

Oliver, too, was dressed in jeans and a blue flannel shirt and wore a full blonde beard. His head was shaved. His eyes had that translucent look to them, with a hint of blue. He did look younger than Pumpernickel but Toby had no idea what younger meant when you live for centuries.

"And this is my cousin, Evy."

Evy had long, brown hair braided into a ponytail, if that's what girls called them here. She wore the same type of clothes, from the jeans to a brown flannel shirt. She had bright brown eyes rather than the translucent ones. She stood about a foot shorter than her cousins.

Evy bowed.

"Evy is honored to meet you," she said.

Toby and Clygon looked around to see who she was talking about.

"She always refers to herself in the third person," Oliver laughed.

"She does," Evy agreed.

"Come with us, friends," Pumpernickel said.

Oliver moved behind them as Pumpernickel and Evy led them deeper into the heart of the mountain. Evy held a bright light to lead the way.

"So… how did you know we were coming?" Toby asked and then answered his own question. "The Christmas Giant!"

Another big, hearty Pumpernickel laugh. "Yes. The Christmas Giant, as you call him. We know him by an ancient name spoken only by the giants. While we grieved his passing, his spirit is alive and well, as you both know."

A groan seeped out of Clygon.

Pumpernickel stopped and stooped down, getting face-to-face with Clygon. It looked like a boulder, speaking to a lumpy bowling ball.

"Clygon! We hold no ill will toward you. Your friend CG has given you his blessing. We can do no less. Come."

After about a twenty-minute walk, Toby thought he could hear what sounded like hammering on metal. Several moments later, he could see something glowing up ahead.

The sound of life grew louder when suddenly the large hallway opened up into a massive underground city. Houses were carved into the walls like a scene out of Petra (he'd seen it in the first *Indiana Jones* movie—one of his dad's favorites). Shops lining streets selling goods to shoppers. Forging fires with giants shaping metal. C-9 Christmas lights hanging everywhere bringing color to what would be a fairly gloomy setting.

In the center of the city stood a huge cauldron. Flumes attached to the top of it conveyed glowing liquid metal to the forges. The cauldron was heated by bright red boulders.

Suddenly, Saaba growled.

"Welcome to Tikvah! The Home of the Giants."

But it wasn't the voice of Pumpernickel. The voice was menacing.

They found themselves surrounded by six armed giants, with swords pointed at them.

7. Giant Hall

"Lucas," Pumpernickel said in a soft voice, his hands held up in a non-threatening manner. Toby couldn't figure out which giant was Lucas.

But it didn't take long. One of the giants took a step toward Pumpernickel and lowered his sword. Unlike Pumpernickel, Oliver, and Evy, Lucas wore the clothes of a warrior—leather pants, a leather vest with his massive, muscular arms exposed, a small dagger—small in giant terms—attached to his right upper arm, the sheath for his sword at his side, and dark brown boots. His dark hair was cut short. His face was set in a frown. The stubble on his face would have been a beard on normal humans. His huge eyes did not look happy. He appeared to be a general or commander of some sort.

"Pumpernickel!" Lucas demanded. "What are these strangers doing here?"

"Lucas…"

But Lucas wasn't done.

"You have violated our ancient code. We withdrew from the world centuries ago for a reason. We have cut ourselves off from strangers like these…" He spit out the words in disgust as he nodded toward Toby, Clygon, and Saaba. "… especially the trolls…"

The anger directed at Clygon almost knocked Clygon over.

"Lucas. This is Toby Baxter. He's brought the Sword to us…"

"Enough, Pumpernickel! Bring them to the High Council."

Pumpernickel turned to Toby and Clygon with a smile and said, "Don't worry. It's a longstanding misunderstanding that we will fix in short order." His words seemed more encouraging than his face.

By now, a group of giants had gathered around to see what the fuss was about. Men. Women. Children… who were already Toby's size.

"Is that Toby Baxter?" he heard someone whisper.

"And he's here with the troll!"

"Is the Prophecy coming true?"

Prophecy?

As the crowd pressed in, Pumpernickel whispered to Toby, "Give me the Sword."

Toby handed his backpack to Pumpernickel, who then handed it to Oliver.

"Get this to the armory and have them assess the damage. Do it quickly," Pumpernickel whispered.

Oliver slipped away just as three of the soldiers moved behind them. Lucas and the other two soldiers led them down a market street, past homes, all the while circling the huge cauldron.

They walked in silence, taking in the magnitude of the city.

Ten minutes later, they were standing in front of a massive door, a huge column on each side, carved into a wall. The top of the door was adorned with carved images—giants, elves, wolves, gnomes, ogres, and, to Toby's surprise, the Sword embedded in the stone just outside of *RiverHome*.

"It's a tribute to when the world lived in harmony," Evy leaned down to whisper.

"Silence!" Lucas demanded.

"Lucas…" Pumpernickel said in a soft voice.

"Save it for the High Council, Pumpernickel."

They walked through the gigantic doors into a giant hall.

"I think that's a homonym," Clygon whispered to Toby.

"Huh?"

"A homonym. When a word can mean two different things."

"I know what a homonym is. I learned about it the first time I was here. But what homonym are you talking about?"

"You were thinking the same thing I was when we walked in. This is a giant hall. Get it? Giant as in big hall and giant as in a giant's hall? A homonym, right?"

"One more word or sound, and I'll have you gagged," Lucas said.

"Another homonym, I think. Gag is a sound, and a gag stops you from making a sound," Clygon whispered and then looked up innocently at Lucas.

In front of them was a high wall behind which sat four massive chairs. Occupying the chairs were four giants—two males and two females. They all wore long gray robes with some sort of silver thing on their heads that looked like leaves. All of them had those translucent eyes, but one of the male giants—who looked a bit like Pumpernickel—had a brightness in his eyes that the others didn't. *That's the nice thing about giants. You can really see their eyes.*

They stopped. Lucas stepped out to address the four.

"High Council. We appreciate your willingness to meet on such short notice. As you can see, *Tikvah* is under a grave threat. Non-giants have somehow, in some way, gotten past our security systems, infiltrated our home, and now pose a great danger to our people."

Three of the High Council leaned forward, concern on their big faces. But the one with the bright eyes smiled and said, "Is that really so, General Lucas? No offense to our guests, but they don't look like they are about to overthrow our people or our home."

Pumpernickel suppressed a chortle.

A chortle?

"To chuckle gleefully," Evy leaned down to whisper to Toby.

"How did you...?"

But Evy quickly stood straight, a passive look on her face. Followed by a quick wink at Toby, along with a small grin. Small for a giant. A full smile for a human.

"Lord Harold, with all due respect. These who stand before you are not guests. They are infiltrators. This is Clygon of the trolls."

An audible gasp from the towns-giants behind them. Apparently, Clygon had quite a reputation.

"Interesting," Lord Harold said. "Yes. Interesting. I am curious as to why a troll is in *Tikvah* and how he got here, but at the same time…"

"If I may, Lord Harold," Pumpernickel interrupted.

Lucas muttered under his breath. But Pumpernickel ignored him.

"Lord Harold. Great Grandfather. Yes, this is Clygon. But as you can see, he is nothing like the Clygon of old. He was sent here by Lord Trut-Vader."

Another audible gasp from the crowd. This time, one of excitement. Lucas took a step back, stunned by the news. Lord Harold let out a huge, deep-belly laugh. The other three council members remained stone-faced.

"The Christmas Giant," Pumpernickel explained to Toby and Clygon. "In Giant, we know him as Lord Trut-Vader—Truth Father."

"Trut-Vader is an old legend!" Lucas shouted. "A myth. A story we tell our kids to make sure they behave."

Pumpernickel turned to Clygon. "Describe him for us, young Clygon."

Clygon stepped forward and bowed to the council.

"We know him as the Christmas Giant," Clygon began. "He has a dark brown beard and brown curly hair with a streak of gray in it. On his head, he wears a wreath of evergreen branches. He's clothed in a long green cloak or robe."

A murmur from the crowd.

"That could be any giant," Lucas protested weakly.

"He smells like Christmas!" Toby shouted. "He has the voice of my grandpa Baxter."

The hall fell silent.

"Sir," Pumpernickel said, "this is Toby Baxter."

This time, the hall exploded into a blend of ahhs, murmurs, and gasps.

Once Lord Harold got control back, he nodded to Clygon.

"Continue."

"Toby is right. He does smell like Christmas. Although I couldn't smell it until recently. I saw him as my enemy. I wanted to destroy him. And I thought I had…"

"We've heard," one of the female council members said angrily.

"He didn't harm him," Toby jumped in. "I see it now. The Christmas Giant breathed out his life into me and Clovor, the Commander of the river elves. He told us he was doing that so that he could always be present with us. I've seen him since then. I've heard him."

"He spoke to me, too," Clygon continued. "He gave me a new start. And he sent me here to… to…" Clygon faltered, looking embarrassed.

"To what, young troll?" Lord Harold asked gently.

"To save you."

Lucas let out a loud, cynical laugh, as did many in the hall.

"You? Save us? The giants? What? With a skinny teenager from another land and a gnome's wolf?"

Saaba bared his teeth and growled. Lucas took another step back.

"This is all a cover for the trolls to bring their violence and hatred into *Tikvah*. This Christmas Giant does not exist. You can't believe a troll!"

"Wow. He really, really does not like you," Toby whispered to Clygon.

"What about the Prophecy?" someone yelled from the crowd.

The crowd joined in.

"What about the Prophecy? What about the Prophecy?" they chanted.

Lord Harold stood up, and the crowd fell silent. He closed his eyes as if seeing what he was saying:

Former enemies they may be…

A human and a troll.

The Sword in peril…

On a Quest they go.

To find the GOOD…

And save the world.

A holy hush fell upon the hall. Something deep in those words spoke to the hearts of the giants. No one moved…

… until…

Toby began to giggle.

Clygon poked him with his elbow.

"What are you doing?" he whispered to Toby.

But Toby couldn't stop himself. He tried to keep it in, but it came out in a loud snort. Soon, his giggling turned to deep belly laughter, causing tears to flow down his cheeks. *Is this a chortle?* Whatever it was, it was infectious, as some of the giants began to giggle along, including one of the giants on the council.

Everyone stared at him. Lucas with disdain. Lord Harold with amusement. Clygon slowly moved away from him.

"I… I… am so… sorry," Toby said through the laughter. "I haven't slept for who knows how long and… when… I'm sleep-deprived… I get… so sorry…"

"What did you find so humorous in the Prophecy, Toby?" asked Lord Harold, seemingly holding in a chortle of his own.

"Don't! Don't answer it," Clygon hissed.

"It's not… it's not the Prophecy… but the…"

"Don't!" Clygon said more urgently.

"Well… the poem wasn't exactly written by Tolkien, was it," Toby said, wiping the tears from his face. *Like I'm some kind of*

Tolkien expert having read The Hobbit! "Sounds like something Yoda would have written." Toby started laughing again.

In the midst of his laughing fit, Toby could feel all the eyes looking up at Lord Harold.

No one moved. No one dared…

…until…

Lord Harold exploded into laughter, almost knocking Toby and Clygon over.

"Toby Baxter… you… are the first… person," he said between laughs, "to say what we all know. That poem is rubbish. Total trash." He paused to catch his breath. "And everyone treats it like a sacred text." He wiped tears from his cheeks.

"Let me tell you something I've never told anyone," he continued. "The Prophecy was given to my father, Lord Theodore, in a world long ago. He entrusted it to me to keep and to pass down to my son and future generations until finally the Prophecy comes to life.

"One night, centuries ago, I had a dream. At least I thought it was a dream. A man sat at the foot of my bed, surrounded by a glow. He was dark of skin with a bright bald head, reading glasses hanging around his neck, a pencil behind his ear, and a small journal in his large hand."

Author? Toby said to himself. *How old are you? You really are a boomer!*

"He recited the Prophecy in the form of that poem. But he didn't just read it. The words he spoke appeared above his head. It was etched in my mind from that night forward. It became a way for all of us to remember it. I always did think that, if whoever that was in my room that night was a writer, he should stick to prose and give up his attempts at poetry. But even though the poem doesn't do it justice, the Prophecy behind it is real, regardless of what unbelievers like Lucas think." He shot a raised eyebrow at Lucas. "It appears that you and Clygon *are* here to save us."

"But… but… your honor… Lord Harold… surely you cannot possibly believe that the fate of the giants is in the hands of these two?"

Just then, Oliver ran into the hall and whispered into Pumpernickel's ear.

"Lord Harold."

It was evident from Pumpernickel's tone that something was wrong.

"The Sword is here."

More gasps.

"But there's a problem…"

8. Story Time

It took a few moments for Oliver and Evy to lead Toby, Clygon, and Saaba through the crowd to a smaller—yet still gigantic—room off of the hall. It reminded Toby of Donold's command centers. The room held an uncomfortable silence due to a tense conversation between Pumpernickel and Lucas.

"Lucas. You grew up with the Prophecy. You felt the Sword break just like I did. You see the shattered Sword in front of you. You know our calling to serve."

Toby noticed the Sword laid out in pieces on a rock table.

"What are the odds that a troll and a human would suddenly show up after the breaking of the Sword? And how else do you think they got here," he said, nodding to Toby, Clygon, and Saaba. "They must have had help. Lord Trut-Vader must have told them or guided them. What are your eyes telling you, Lucas? The Prophecy is in play. And we need to help them."

"No! This is a ploy by our enemies. We have made many sacrifices to live apart from the violence and terror and war of the rest of the world. We will not allow *creatures* like them into our home. It will destroy us."

A number of giants who had followed them grunted their agreement. This felt like a long-standing division in giant land.

Lucas turned to go when Pumpernickel put his hand out and touched Lucas's arm. "Wait, Lucas. Let's at least hear what the problem is with the Sword and what Toby and Clygon have to say for themselves. If the Prophecy is coming true, don't you want to be a part of it?"

Lucas pulled his arm away, turned, and marched out of the room. Several giants followed.

"He's always been hot-headed." Lord Harold entered the room with one of the other council members. "His *Giants-Only* ideology has clouded his otherwise sharp mind." He shook his head.

Turning to Toby, Clygon, and Saaba, he said, "On behalf of all of *Tikvah*, I apologize for the rudeness of Lucas. We are a people of friendship. We never use weapons to harm, only to heal and bring about peace. I'm deeply embarrassed that he and his soldiers pointed their swords at you. That is not who we are." His shoulders sank.

After a moment, he headed over to the table holding the Sword and invited the others to join him.

The Sword was laid out in the same way as Clovor had done in the hotel room in Maui. *Are my parents and Sid back at the hotel by now? Are they worried about me?*

"Tell us the story of how the Sword came to be like this," Lord Harold said.

Toby gave a brief overview of his first visit to *RiverHome* and how he had planted the Sword at Clygon's stronghold to act as a barrier.

Clygon picked up the story from there.

"The Sword served its purpose well. Those of us who intended harm on the river elves and their friends were rebuffed by the Sword. If we tried to cross its line, we were met with a rather shocking shock. The longer it held, the angrier I became."

"Wait," Toby interrupted. "How do you remember all of that? You became a baby…"

Clygon smiled.

"I de-aged, Toby, but I didn't lose my memories."

Clygon paused to re-collect his thoughts. *Apparently he lost them when I interrupted him!*

"But then, years later, we noticed that the shock was not as shocking. The light of the Sword began to dim. Finally, I had had enough. I walked out and put my hands on the hilt of the Sword, determined to get it to drain its energy into me. But it… it just… exploded into pieces. It broke."

Pumpernickel smiled. "It did exactly as it was designed to do when it was losing its strength."

"I couldn't believe it," Clygon continued. "The barrier was gone. We were free to go where we pleased. I picked up the pieces and put them in a sack, assuming that if nothing else, I could show that child Toby Baxter—sorry Toby—that his power was gone. He beat me once. He wouldn't beat me a second time. But—"

"But I had *Loach,*" Toby jumped in. "The elves brought me back to *RiverHome* to use *Loach* as a backup until they could figure out what had happened to the Sword. Using *Loach,* my dad and I were able to defeat that monster Clygon—sorry Clygon—and here we are. Apparently, the two enemies of the Prophecy."

Lord Harold waved his hand over the Sword. It sparked to life and began to glow. "We have the magic to repair it. And we've no time to waste as we can feel *Loach* losing its power. But... someone said there's a problem?"

A giant in a long white scientist coat stepped forward. Her name badge read *Rainie*. Toby gasped.

"What is it, son?" Pumpernickel asked.

"I... ah... well... there's this Rainie I... ah.... know back home...."

He knew his face was beet red.

"Never mind."

Clygon snickered, and everyone around the table laughed along. Rainie winked at him, making him all the more embarrassed.

She pointed at the Sword. "In order to restore the Sword, we need every single piece. If even the tiniest of pieces is missing, we can't put it back together. And we can't add in a new piece. It would mess with the integrity of its power and magic."

"Are you saying something is missing?" Lord Harold asked.

"Wait... what? Clovor laid out the Sword in our hotel room in Hawaii."

They all looked at him.

"Long story. She said it would be a miracle if all of the Sword pieces were still there. She was confident they were. Are you saying she missed something?

"She's not to be faulted. We didn't see it at first, either. Let me show you. Toby… wave your hand over the Sword."

Toby stifled a yawn and then stepped up and held his hand over the Sword. He could feel some of its energy flowing into him. But it was much weaker than before. He ran his hand from the hilt to the tip, and as he did, it began to glow once again. But this time, he saw something he'd never seen before. Writing. At least he assumed it was writing, although in a script and language he couldn't read.

"The Sword," Rainie continued, "is empowered by words, seven power words, to be precise. And if one word is missing, or even a few letters of one of the words, the Sword cannot be healed. Here. Look."

She waved her hand over the Sword, and the script turned to English.

"What words do you see Toby?"

He and Clygon bumped heads as they both leaned down over the Sword.

"HERO," Toby pointed. "WISE… Wait, each time I've been here I've had a compass using those words."

"LOVE. HOPE. TRUE. GRIT." Clygon pointed at each.

Toby rubbed his eyes. He was having a hard time keeping them open. Near the tip of the Sword, he spotted a G. The rest of the word was gone. But he knew what it was supposed to say.

"GOOD. The GOOD is missing. That's why the Prophecy said we are to find the GOOD."

"Correct, Toby," Rainie said. "But the piece is so small you wouldn't notice it if you couldn't read the words. That's why Clovor missed…"

The next thing he knew, he was in a huge bed, with Saaba snuggled up next to him and Clygon in the bed across the room, snoring so loudly that the room was shaking. He heard a movement in the corner, and Pumpernickel stood up and walked over to him.

"What happened? How did I get here?"

Pumpernickel chuckled.

"You fell asleep right in the middle of a sentence. You were also pretty dehydrated, so while you were sleeping, Rainie nursed some hydrating lemon juice—a giant specialty—into you. And the stalagmite stings didn't help, either. If you're hungry, let's go and get you some food. We'll wake Rumpelstiltskin over there," he nodded toward Clygon, "as soon as we need to get moving. We suspect Lucas is hatching a plan to stop you."

"Why? And why don't you stop him?"

"It's a complicated mess, to be honest. Lucas represents a large group of giants who want nothing to do with the outside world, no matter what the outside world does to itself. *Giants-Only!* They live in fear, Toby. And fear isolates and makes enemies. The giant way is the way of peace, friendship, and service. Some of us have lost our way. We're trying to avoid a civil war."

As they turned to go, Rumpelstiltskin woke up.

"Hey, wait for me. I'm starving."

Lord Harold, Oliver, Evy, and Rainie were sitting at a large table. Toby and Clygon did their best to climb up onto two of the empty stools, their heads barely reaching over the tabletop.

"Cheerios or Fruit Loops?" asked Rainie.

Instead of using giant bowls, she used tea cups for the cereal, which were about the size of a human bowl.

They both ate three cups of cereal. Saaba, too, ate his fill of dog food. They all got a good laugh hearing Toby's retelling of how Clygon was "reborn," and broke into several Christmas songs to see if they would de-age Clygon once again. But Clygon had grown to appreciate Christmas music and sang along.

After they were done eating, Lord Harold said, "Come. Time is short. And we have much to tell you."

He led them down a hallway back into the small room holding the lifeless Sword.

Some small-ish giant children chairs had been brought in for Toby and Clygon to sit on.

Lord Harold and the other giants sat down.

"Let me tell you a story."

Lord Harold began to hum—the same Celtic-type sound used by the river elves when they told stories. *Enya strikes again!*

"For tens of thousands of years after the Creator spoke life into being, the creatures of the land, sea, and air lived in harmony. Trolls, gnomes, ogres, elves, giants, humans, and all the peoples of the earth lived as neighbors, tilling the land, sharing food, caring for one another's children, sharing stories…"

"That's almost exactly the way Deckor tells the story," Clygon said excitedly to Toby.

"That's how he told it to me, too!"

"And then," Lord Harold continued, "the Chaos descended over the earth. A darkness one could not see, only feel. A foreboding. A terror. A fear. An undefined sense of despair that slowly began to breed suspicion and distrust between neighbors. The trolls moved to the east. The ogres migrated south. The elves to the west. And the humans to the north. No one knew why. It was all instinct. Perhaps it was fear bred by distrust.

"From the very beginning of existence, we knew our role in creation—to bring peace. To maintain harmony. But the violence and distrust and hatred around us overwhelmed us. In our own despair, we, and I say this to our shame, we decided to withdraw from the world. Rather than trying to be a force for good, we looked for a place to hide. As far as the outside world was concerned, we vanished."

The volume of the humming softened. Lord Harold stared off into the distance.

"The Sword," Toby said. "What about the Sword?"

Pumpernickel spoke, or sang, or whatever.

"As Lord Harold said, many of us felt deep shame for abandoning the world. It's hard to explain, my new friends, but the Chaos and the resulting violence caused us physical pain. We felt we had no choice but to withdraw from the land above. In our despair, Lord Trut-Vader—the Christmas Giant—had a vision of how we might atone for our guilt. In these mountains, we discovered a rare form of metal. Lord Trut-Vader, in his vision, saw a way for us to forge that metal into a Sword that might help bring peace. After centuries of failures…"

"Centuries? Just how old is the Christmas Giant?" Toby asked in awe.

"Older than the ancient trees in your world," Pumpernickel answered with a wink. "After centuries of failure, we were finally able to forge the Sword—a weapon that would give and protect life rather than destroy it. All of our passion and goodwill was poured into the making of that Sword. We created a backup—*Loach*. Like your NFL backup quarterbacks," Pumpernickel winked again at Toby. "*Loach* was meant to fill the void, should there be one, for a short period of time.

"We held onto this technology for hundreds of years. But the shame of watching from the sidelines as the world ripped itself apart deepened. Finally, we reached out to the leaders of *RiverHome* and entrusted them with the Sword and *Loach*, much to their shock. They thought we had disappeared."

"So… that means… that the river elves believe that you re-disappeared, if that's a word," Toby said. *Could I add another that into that sentence? Wait, I just did!*

"Let's just say that after handing off *Loach* to the river elves we used a little giant magic to help them forget to remember us." Pumpernickel shook his head. "Anyway, they, in turn, eventually entrusted the Baxter family with *Loach* for its safekeeping."

Passion… heart… metal… unite!

Forge a Sword!

Protect with Light!

Toby put his hands over his mouth as everyone turned to look at him.

Where did that come from? Author!

"If you think poetry is in your future, I wouldn't drop out of school just yet if I were you," Clygon said.

Pumpernickel laughed. "Well… it does summarize the story."

Lord Harold looked at him. "It sounds like you might know the author of my Prophecy poem?" He grinned at Toby as he said it.

In addition to that lame Author-inspired poem, Toby had a myriad of questions buzzing around in his head. *Or maybe it was a rogue stalagmite?*

"Why not make more swords like the Sword? Why not plant them throughout the land?"

"Good questions, Toby," Lord Harold responded. "For some reason, we have not been able to replicate the magic, so to speak, of the Sword. We've been able to fashion swords, swords that are far superior to any of those in the world above us. But not one that works, not as a weapon of destruction, but as a source of life like the Sword. The Prophecy specifically focuses on the Sword, not on creating new Swords."

"Okay… but… why… why don't you leave the mountains and enter back into the outside world? If you have the ability to help bring peace to the world, why are you still here?"

Suddenly, they heard the unsheathing of swords.

"Because the outside world will taint us. It will pervert us as it has itself. We must protect ourselves!"

It was Lucas.

"Take them away."

9. Uprising

"Lucas, what is the meaning of this?" demanded Lord Harold.

"They," Lucas responded, pointing his sword in the direction of Toby, Clygon, and Saaba, "are what *this* is about. It's one thing to live in the past, wishing for a world that no longer exists and our place in it. But when the world starts coming in here, threatening our safety, our way of life, our children, then enough is enough. I am relieving you of duty and taking on the role of Lord of the Giants."

Lucas spat out the words, some of which landed on Toby, forcing him to take a few steps back. *Giant spit is ginormous!* It felt like a shower.

"By whose authority?" Lord Harold was incredulous. *That's a big word.*

Lucas made a brief nod of his head, and twenty armed giants, with what looked like hundreds of towns-giants behind them, moved into sight.

"Lucas," Pumpernickel said, "we are giants. We are creatures of peace. This is not who we are. This action undoes all that we stand for. Let's talk this through, Lucas, as we always do. The Prophecy…"

"The Prophecy is the mindless babblings of old, foolish giants. We will not allow their ramblings to deceive us into our own demise."

"But—"

Lucas cut him off with another nod of his head, which resulted in the twenty armed giants surrounding Toby, Clygon, Saaba, Pumpernickel, Lord Harold—apparently now just Harold—Oliver, Evy, and Rainie.

As they started to move, Toby noticed out of the corner of his eye—*but eyes are almond-shaped. How can they have corners?*—Rainie handing what, in her hands, looked like a small bag to Pumpernickel. Pumpernickel slid it under his shirt. It was the Sword. He nodded at Toby.

"No worries, Toby," he whispered. "This story is just getting started."

They were marched through the center of the city, crowds lining the streets. Some of them booed as they passed by, but most simply lowered their eyes as if embarrassed. More likely afraid. Or intimidated.

They eventually stopped at what appeared to be a large home carved into the mountain wall.

"We will treat you with courtesy for your years of service, Harold," growled Lucas. "You will be well fed. You will be protected. But none of you will be allowed out of this house until we have decided what we will do with those three," nodding toward Toby, Clygon, and Saaba, "and until we set up a new government. We will have guards stationed outside these doors at all times."

With that, Lucas turned and marched off to the cheers of *Giants Only! Giants Only!*

A giantess stood in the huge hallway of the house. She had long, gray hair, light blue translucent eyes, a friendly-looking face, and wore what looked like clothes from the 1970s—bell-bottom jeans and a paisley blouse with large, balloon-type sleeves. Toby had seen pictures from that era of his grandparents when they were teenagers wearing clothes like that. For some reason, the word *groovy* came to mind.

Harold rushed up to her, and the two of them hugged to the point where Toby felt a bit embarrassed. She looked at him over Harold's shoulder and gave him a huge smile. It reminded him a bit of the Christmas Giant.

"Harold, please introduce me to your guests."

Harold turned and, with his arm around her waist, said, "Toby, Clygon, and Saaba, this is my wife, Chantelle. Chantelle, this is the troll, Clygon, the wolf, Saaba, and *the* Toby Baxter."

Chantelle stooped down a bit, reached out her big hand, and shook the hands of Toby and Clygon, while scratching a sweet spot under Saaba's right ear.

She turned to the other giants and said, "Come on in, everyone. It looks like Lucas is having another one of his temper tantrums." But her humor didn't seem all that humorous. Her big giant face showed concern.

Pumpernickel closed the doors behind them as they headed into a large—*of course it's large*—living room. A fire in the corner filled the room with warmth, and the lighting made it feel like daytime.

They all took seats. Clygon and Toby had to climb a bit to get onto the couch. They sat in silence for what seemed like several minutes, watching as Chantelle and Harold brought out large—*again, of course they would be large*—plates of food. But no one really felt like eating.

Harold took a seat.

"I don't think we have much time. We need to get ahead of Lucas. Our first priority is to help Toby, Clygon, and Saaba find the GOOD, heal the Sword, and get it back to *RiverHome*. Toby. Clygon. Any thoughts on where the GOOD might be?"

"I can think of two places," Clygon said glumly. "The first is at my former stronghold, where Toby first buried the Sword. Or… I guess it could be at *Ogreton Heights,* where the fragments spilled onto the floor of that hall when Toby ambushed me with Christmas songs."

"Pa Rum Pum Pum Pum…" Toby sang.

"But my hunch is the stronghold," Clygon continued. "And once we find it, then what? How do we restore the Sword's power? And where is the Sword, by the way?"

Pumpernickel pulled the Sword-in-the-bag out from under his shirt. As he did so, Rainie pulled a small vile out of hers.

"This," she said, "is the last bit of metal we have from the creation of the Sword. We've been able to keep it in its liquid form but once exposed to the air, it will harden and will be of no use. When you find the GOOD, you will need to lay out the Sword with the missing piece and put a touch of this liquid on the hilt and the point. It will bring the Sword fully back to life. But," she said with a warning in her voice, "you will only get one chance."

"No pressure," Toby muttered.

Suddenly, they heard the sound of sword against sword outside of the house.

"Quickly, we need to get them out of here," Harold said, jumping to his large feet. "Pumpernickel, take them to the back, to the secret hallway. Toby, come with me."

As Pumpernickel led Clygon and Saaba out of the living room, Harold rushed Toby into a side bedroom. Harold ran over to a picture on the wall. *The Christmas Giant!* He pushed on it, and the picture moved, revealing a safe. Harold quickly opened it and pulled out a small bag."

"Here, Toby, take this. It will guide you."

Toby opened the bag and discovered a compass—the same compass from his first trip to *RiverHome!* The same compass from his second adventure as well. He opened it, and once again, rather than N-E-S-W, the coordinates spelled a word. Not surprisingly, like H-E-R-O from the first visit and W-I-S-E from the second, this time, the coordinates read: G-O-O-D.

"What do the letters mean? The last two times, the letters stood for words that led me to where I needed to be."

"I'm sorry, Toby. I have no idea. You will have to discover their meaning as you discover your way."

"But… that's impossible! How do I know where I'm going if I don't know where I'm going?"

Harold put his massive hands on Toby's shoulders.

"Toby, the whole purpose of a Quest is to forge you into a HERO—a WISE, GOOD man. In this case, you will have to discover for yourself what it means to be GOOD as you try to save us and *RiverHome.*"

The noise had moved into the house.

"Where are they?" a voice demanded.

"Trolls?" Harold and Toby said at the same time.

"Harold!" It was Chantelle, the panic in her voice causing the hair on the back of Toby's neck to go up.

"Go, Toby!" Harold said. "Out this way. Pumpernickel will help you."

"But what about you? What about the giants?"

"Our story is now in your hands, Toby Baxter. Find the GOOD. Now go!"

Toby ran in the direction Harold pointed, out a small—small for giants—door into a long hallway. Up ahead, he could see light. Then he saw Pumpernickel.

"Toby, I've already fitted Clygon with some supplies. Oliver and Evy will go with you. No time to waste, my young friend."

"But… will I see you again?" Toby asked.

Pumpernickel smiled.

"That, my friend, is yet to be written."

Good grief! He sounds like Author.

"And protect this."

Pumpernickel handed Toby the Sword-in-the-bag. Toby stuffed it into the backpack also handed to him by Pumpernickel.

"Come! Now!" Oliver demanded.

They stepped out of the back hallway and once again into the bowels of *Tikvah*.

10. A Narrow Escape

They walked quietly through the huge hallways of the mountain. Oliver took the lead, and Evy took the rear. Toby noticed that Saaba had a pack of some sort attached to his back. Food, no doubt.

"What's the source of your light?" Toby asked Oliver. Oliver held what looked like a small sword in his hand. Instead of a tip, it had a small orb that radiated light, not unlike the *Elf Orb* Clygon had given to him, but much smaller and much brighter.

"Each of these orbs is forged out of a special crystal we discovered centuries ago. Using extremely high pressure, we fashion the crystal into this ball-like orb. It lasts for years before we have to change it out."

"How do you turn it on and off… or dim it?" Clygon asked.

Oliver stopped and showed them his light.

"See this small button just above the hilt? When I press it up, a small piece of metal slides into the crystal and dims the light. If I push the metal piece all the way in, it shuts the light off. I'm not a scientist, like Rainie, but somehow the metal absorbs the light and then releases the light back into the orb when I push the button down."

Clygon and Oliver fell into a conversation about their orb lights, which Toby found boring and a bit geeky. Saaba slipped up next to him, and the two of them walked side by side, one mundane step after another. Occasionally, Toby would hear a sound reverberating around the rock walls and would instinctively duck. But it always turned out to be nothing. Or so he hoped.

"Evy is hungry," Evy said from behind them.

"Evy is always hungry," Oliver answered back with a laugh. "But Oliver... er... I'm hungry, too, and I'm guessing you guys are, as well."

They walked on for another five minutes and finally stopped at a spot that looked like a small room. Off to the side, a bit down another hallway, was what looked like a bench. Toby was hoping he wouldn't need it. Off to the other side was a small indentation where Oliver began to build a small fire. The draft from the hole above took the smoke up so that it didn't fill in the area around them.

Saaba ran off for a few moments and came back, seemingly satisfied that all was safe.

"No need to worry, Saaba," Evy said. "No one knows these halls exist except us giants. You're safe here."

Saaba walked in a circle five times and then curled up in a ball and promptly fell asleep... although one eye remained open.

Whatever Oliver was cooking smelled delicious. Toby could feel his mouth watering. Next to him Clygon was playing with Oliver's sword light, constantly turning it on and off, and marveling at its engineering with oohs and aahs.

Moments later, seated around the fire, Oliver served them some amazingly tasty grilled vegetables.

"How in the world do you grow vegetables in a mountain?" Toby asked with a mouthful of now mushy asparaguses. *Or is it asparagi?*

"Evy can answer that," Evy said. "One of Evy's jobs is to oversee our food supply. It's a calling handed down to me from one of my ancestors to the next over many, many centuries. We begin with…"

"I'm pretty sure they were just being polite, Evy, and aren't really all that interested in giant agriculture."

Evy didn't seem to be put out.

"But there must be some things you are interested in?" she asked Toby and Clygon. "After all, you are the first non-giants in this place in recent memory, which for us goes back to the Chaos."

"Well… now that you ask. Is it really true that you have not been out of the mountain ever in your life?" Clygon asked.

"Not once," Oliver answered. "We can't take the risk of being spotted. Right or wrong, we have chosen to live apart from the world. To live in peace. To live above—or in this case, below—the unrest and hatred and violence unleashed by the Chaos."

Toby noticed Oliver shaking his head.

"But… you don't agree with that decision?" he asked the giant.

Oliver and Evy looked at each other.

"Evy will answer. Evy and Oliver believe that we should engage with the world. That we should live out our calling as peacemakers. We have much we can offer. Yes. It is a risk. Yes. We could lose our peaceful way of living. But this way of life is not what the Creator created us for."

"Obviously Lucas disagr—" Clygon started to say.

Oliver held a hand up. He put a finger to his lips to silence them. Saaba's head shot up.

They sat still for several moments listening.

Then Toby heard it. Faint at first. It sounded similar to when he rode his bike on wet streets. But as the sound grew louder it sounded like something moving its way through slime. Or… snot. The sound was grotesque.

"Stalactites!" Oliver, Evy, and Clygon shouted at the same time.

"Stalactites?" Toby asked. "Aren't they…"

"They are big, fat, round balls of squishy gelatin that suck up everything in their path. If that thing in their path is living, it sucks the very breath out of them," Oliver said. "And to make matters worse, they fill in every crack and space in their way. They are impossible to escape," he said as he was dampening the fire and packing up the gear.

"We need to run. Now!"

"But they can't be fast, can they?"

"Put on your backpack and run, Toby! Run!"

Oliver and Evy flicked on their orbs to help them see. Once again, Toby was grateful for the large hallways, ensuring he wouldn't bump his head.

They ran deeper into the mountain. They turned left. They turned right. But the sound kept getting closer. And more disgusting. It sounded like a giant with a severe head cold.

Then Toby felt a change. They were headed up.

"No, Oliver! We can't!"

"There is no other choice, Evy. We have to protect the Sword."

They kept running. Toby's legs were killing him. It was getting harder and harder to breathe, especially now running uphill.

"They're… gaining on… us, Oliver," Evy yelled. We're not… going to… make… it."

"I have… a… plan…" Oliver yelled as best as he could.

Suddenly, Oliver stopped. Clygon ran into him. Toby ran into Clygon. Evy almost stepped on Toby. Saaba slid in between and placed himself next to Toby. They were all doubled over, trying to catch their breath.

The mucusy-sounding stalactites were closing in on them. Not only did they sound disgusting, but now Toby could smell them. He started to dry heave.

"Hold yourself together, Toby. We have one shot to survive this."

Oliver started running again. Higher and higher they went.

Then he stopped. The hallway had run out of hallway. They hit a dead end.

"You're… not seriously… thinking…" Evy said between breaths.

"Do you… have a better… idea?"

She shook her head.

"Evy does not… have a… better idea."

"Whatever… it is…" Toby said. "We're… in!"

"Get behind me," Oliver yelled.

Toby, Clygon, and Saaba moved behind Oliver and Evy. The two giants now served as a wall between Toby, Clygon, Saaba, and the oncoming stalactite.

"Wait!" Toby yelled. "You're not sacrificing your lives for us! There has to be another way."

Oliver turned and looked at him.

"It's okay, young Toby. Hang on. And if we get separated, find the GOOD!"

Oliver turned back to the quickly approaching stalactite. Toby poked his head around Oliver's massive back and saw a huge ball of blubber coming toward them… sticky, oozy stuff with dust all around it. He could see immediately that it did indeed tightly fill every inch of every space, sucking up everything in front of it, above it, and around it. The smell almost knocked him out.

"Now!" Oliver yelled to Evy.

Oliver and Evy pointed their lights at the stalactite and put them on full beam. The stalactite screamed... *screamed?*... but kept coming toward them. It rolled right into the orbs and slowed. Toby could see the light shining throughout its hideous gelatin body. Inside of it was all kinds of gross stuff.

But it kept moving forward. Oliver and Evy held out as long as they could.

"Toby," Oliver yelled, "when I give the word, you three move off to the sides as best you can."

They waited. The force of the stalactite was pushing the giants into Toby, Clygon, and Saaba, so that they were being squished between the giants and the back wall. Toby was having a hard time breathing.

"Now!" Oliver yelled.

At once, all of them parted to the left or right as best they could. The stalactite, with no more pressure, burst in between them...

... but rather than sucking them all up...

... it hit the back wall and...

... burst through it into daylight...

... exploding into fragments of goop...

...sending Toby, Clygon, Saaba, Oliver, and Evy flying out of the mountain onto a grassy hill...

.... into a group of trolls...

…and…

Lucas?

11. Apparently Not Such a Narrow Escape

The sunlight was blinding after having been in a cave for over a day. But as his eyes adjusted, Toby took in several things at once.

Off to his right, Oliver lay on the ground, his arm over his eyes, moaning in pain. To his left, he saw Evy in a similar position, trying to protect her eyes. As he lifted his head and squinted, he could see Clygon struggling to get from his knees to his feet.

Standing over all of them were three trolls, licking their fingers, seemingly enjoying the stalactite goop that had exploded over all of them.

And standing at his head was Lucas. Clean as can be. Wearing what looked like expensive sunglasses and a hooded cloak to protect him from the sun. The goop must have missed him.

Saaba was nowhere to be found.

"Here," Lucas said as he handed sunglasses to Oliver and Evy. "I always carry spares just in case."

"How... how did you... know... we... would be here?" Toby asked, wiping disgusting stalactite mucus from his mouth.

"I didn't. It was... what's the word... kismet."

"Kisswhat?" Toby asked. *Another word I'll have to Google.*

"He's here to guard the entryway," Oliver said, putting on the sunglasses.

"What entryway?" Clygon asked, finally on his feet and wobbling over to Toby to help him up.

"Do you want me to tell them?" Lucas asked, but not in a polite way. He was taunting Oliver and Evy.

"This is an ancient entryway into the mountain," Lucas decided to answer anyway. "I brought these three," he pointed with his head to the three trolls, "to stand guard over it. Since our home has been breached, we can't stand by and let it happen again."

"So that's why you did what you did?" Toby asked Oliver. "Because you knew it was a way out? That the ancient door might burst under the pressure? Wow... good thinking!"

But Oliver didn't have time to acknowledge him.

"So... you're in league with the trolls now? So much for your *Giants Only* policies!" Evy snarled at Lucas. She tried to jump up and confront him, but she slipped in stalactite pus and fell onto her butt... hard.

"Let's just say we have finally come to an agreement, one I confess I've been working on for some time for such a time as this. We want to keep the world out. The trolls want the Sword. Seems like we can help each other, don't you think?"

Clygon looked at the three trolls, still busy licking the stalactite goop off of themselves and still enjoying it.

"Do I know you?" Clygon snarled.

One of the trolls stepped forward. Like most of the trolls Toby had encountered, this troll was squat and wide, with dark straw-like hair growing every which way all over his rough-skinned body. The nose hairs were particularly disgusting on this one. A small squirrel could swing from them. He wore some sort of fur cloak. Over his shoulder, he carried what Toby assumed was some kind of weapon. The troll had that familiar troll vomit-sweat smell, now mixed with the noxious stalactite odor. The other two trolls looked almost identical to him.

"I'm Hythron." He mockingly bowed to Clygon. "And this is my younger brother Hythron." The second troll bowed. "And this is our younger brother, Hythron." The third brother bowed.

"You all have the same name? That's... that's..." Toby said.

"Dumb!" Oliver said.

"Brilliant!" Hythron #1 said at the exact same time. "Made it easier for our mom to remember our names!"

"Yes," Clygon said. "I remember your family. Not big on the smarts, but well-respected for your muscle!"

The three Hythrons bowed, taking Clygon's remark as a compliment, but what Toby was sure, from the tone of Clygon's voice, was an insult. Or maybe they liked insults.

"Do you know who I am?" Clygon asked.

The three Hythrons moved closer.

"Do you recognize him?" Hythron #2 asked his brothers.

"Nope," answered #3.

"I don't think so," mocked #1.

Toby could see the irritation growing on Clygon's face.

Clygon stood straight.

"I'm Clygon!"

The three brothers took a step back, seeming to recognize who stood before them.

And then… they broke into huge belly laughs. Tears streamed down their faces. Hythron #1 bent over, barely able to breathe.

"We're… so… sorry… your excellency…" laughed Hythron #3.

"Actually," giggled Hythron #2, "we're not."

Clygon looked ready to pounce. But then he shrugged his shoulders.

"Did I smell that bad?" he asked Toby.

"Worse," Toby said.

"Nice chat everyone," Lucas said, "but I have a new governing body to oversee, giants resistant to our cause to lock up, and now need to figure out what to do with the four of you."

Toby noticed the sky starting to gray as clouds began to fill the sky. It was then that he realized that they were high up on a mountain. Around him, he noticed what looked like giant ancient ruins. *Perhaps the ruins from when the giants lived above the ground?* He could see a valley below and what looked like a glimmer of a river. *The River Glaedaan?*

The wind picked up, signaling the approach of a storm.

"We're not going to get down the hill before this storm hits," Oliver yelled through the increasingly strong winds. "We need shelter."

Lucas nodded.

"You three!" he said to the Hythrons. "There's a small enclosure just off to your right that will give you shelter while providing a view of the area. You can stand watch over there until I can send some giants up to close up this entrance."

The Hythrons headed off to their post.

"You four, if you give me your word of no funny stuff, can join me in the mountain as we ride out the storm, rather than out here. We'll spend the night and then head back down tomorrow, stopping along the way to check out the other entrance."

"The other entrance?" Toby whispered to Oliver.

"We have three total, but we only use one when absolutely necessary. This one here and the one down below have been sealed for centuries."

Big drops of rain began to pelt them. So they dived back through the mountain entrance and walked down the slippery-from-the-stalactite-goop path some distance until they found a more open area suitable for a fire, for sleeping, and for calls of nature.

They ate in silence. The food provided by the giants made a super-sized drink or extra-large fries look small. But the food was actually quite good. And Toby was hungry.

As they settled in for the night, Lucas said, "Oh, by the way, so I don't forget…" At this, he chuckled as if making a joke, "… I believe you have something I need, Toby Baxter. Could you please hand me the Sword? I need to deliver it to Plythar tomorrow."

"You're actually going to give the Sword to the trolls?" The tone of Clygon's voice suggested he was incredulous. *There's that big word again.*

"Of course. Why not. It's useless. It's missing a piece, and there's no way it will ever be found. But Plythar doesn't need to know that. We'll let him waste his time trying to get the Sword to work again while his trolls help make sure that no one ever enters our home again!"

Toby rolled over in his sleeping bag, trying to ignore him. But Lucas loudly cleared his throat.

"The Sword, Toby! Now! Or I just might have to get a bit nasty. And Oliver and Evy know what I'm like when I'm nasty."

"Evy says just give it to him," Evy said.

"But…"

"Toby," Oliver said quietly. "Give him the Sword."

Toby dug into his backpack and pulled out the leather bag holding the broken Sword. He reluctantly handed it over to Lucas, then turned and covered his head with his pillow.

Now what will I do? No Sword. No river elf friends to help. And no Saaba.

And that was his last thought as he fell asleep.

Where's Saaba?"

Except that that wasn't the last thought. He had one more last thought. A last last thought.

When he had handed the Sword bag to Lucas he noticed that the Sword didn't give off a glow.

12. The Hills are Alive!

Toby slept well. Better than well. He felt more rested than he had for however long he had been in the mountain.

He noticed movement to his left and saw Clygon climbing out of his sleeping bag. He seemed to whisper something to Oliver, nodding to the backpack on Clygon's sleeping bag.

"If you have something to say," Lucas said, "then say it so that I can hear it. We're all friends here. We don't need any secrets."

"I was simply telling Oliver that whatever it is you are cooking for breakfast smells absolutely delicious," Clygon said.

"Uh huh," Lucas answered, not believing a word of it.

But it did smell good. Like bacon and eggs. Which is exactly what Lucas was cooking. Along with waffles. *Where did that stuff come from? Giant magic?*

"We have a long trek ahead of us, and of course, you'll have a long time in prison, so I thought one last good meal would be much appreciated," Lucas said over his shoulder.

Toby got up. He stretched. Then headed to the latrine. Clygon met him there.

"Um... ah... would it be possible to have a bit of privacy?" Toby asked.

"Of course. I just wanted to say, be ready."

"For what?"

"Didn't I say that if you have anything to say you say it out loud?" Lucas shouted.

"Wow. His hearing is amazing!" Toby whispered.

"I have big ears," Lucas deadpanned.

The food tasted as good as it smelled. Lucas seemed to enjoy playing the part of the host but Toby could feel the anger radiating off of Oliver and Evy every time Lucas tried to talk to them.

After breakfast, they packed up their gear. Clygon quickly and quietly handed Toby a tiny, soft pouch. He mimicked putting it in his pocket, so that's what Toby did.

"Now that everyone has had a good rest and is well fed, no more delays. If you would follow me please." Lucas pointed down the hallway leading back into the bowels of *Tikvah*.

Clygon cleared his throat in an obvious attempt to get Lucas's attention.

"What is it, troll?" Lucas was clearly running out of patience.

"Knowing trolls as I do," Clygon said, "I suggest you might want to take a peek outside and make sure those not-so-sharp trolls are still there. It sounded like a pretty violent storm last night."

Toby hadn't heard anything as he'd slept so deeply.

Lucas stared at Clygon for a moment.

"I'm not sure what you're up to, troll, but I suspect you are right. No funny business. Let's go."

Clygon moved as close to Toby as he possibly could and whispered, "When Oliver begins to cough, pull out the pouch, shake it out, jump onto it, and hang on for dear life!"

Lucas turned to look at them before Toby could ask Clygon the six questions that instantly came to mind.

The sky was still overcast, but the storm had passed. The three giants immediately put on their sunglasses to protect their eyes from the brightness.

One of the Hythrons emerged out of the enclosure where they had spent the night. Toby couldn't tell which of the Hythrons this one was.

"Didn't trust us, did you?" Hythron sneered. "I'll bet that snake Clygon tried to tell you we—"

"He did," Lucas cut him off, obviously in a hurry. "Here. I've brought you some food…" He threw a bag of leftovers to Hythron, who quickly hid it so that his brothers wouldn't see it.

"Now…" Lucas turned to the group. "No more delays…"

At that moment, Oliver started to cough. His entire body shook. It looked like he was about to spit out a lung. Evy quickly moved over to him.

"He can't breathe!" she yelled.

Lucas turned to see what was happening.

"Now!" Clygon yelled as he pulled the small pouch out of his pocket, shaking it open as he did. It morphed into what looked to Toby like a blanket or a carpet… but it was moving!

As Clygon jumped onto it, he screamed for Toby to act.

By now, Lucas was onto them and rushed at Toby. Thankfully, Evy tripped him. Were it not for Toby pulling out the pouch, shaking it out, and jumping onto it, Lucas would have fallen on top of him.

Whatever he was sitting on seemingly floated down the hill. It reminded him of riding an inner tube down a big water slide. He grabbed onto the edges as it raced down the mountain.

In moments, he was alongside Clygon. It was then that he saw thousands of little legs underneath the carpet, running down the hill.

"What is this thing?" Toby shouted.

"It's a centipede," Clygon shouted back. "Some of our ogre friends developed it. We had no idea if they actually worked. Woo hoo!"

Toby's centipede took a sharp left, barely missing a tree, only to make a sharp right, barely missing a huge boulder jutting out of the side of the mountain.

"Keep alert," Clygon shouted. "These mountains are alive!"

"What does that mean?"

The answer came a moment later.

Suddenly they were pelted by small stones. The stones flew at Toby and Clygon from all directions.

"Keep your head down, Toby! Trust the centipede!"

"What's going on? Who's throwing stones at us?"

"Those are rock badgers. Small badger-like creatures that badger you for entering their space."

A rock badger hit Toby right above the eye while another hit him on the wrist and yet another on his cheek.

He ducked. More rock badgers flew over his head, barely missing him.

And that's when he heard whispers. They sounded like… *insults?*

Clygon must have heard it too.

"When they can't hit you directly, they badger you with insults. Hang on. We're almost out of their range."

They continued to glide down the mountain, dodging trees, boulders, and rock badgers. Moments later, the rock badgers stopped badgering them. Toby carefully lifted his head, only to be hit by a horrific smell. Worse than troll odor. More noxious than stalactite goop. Toby was pretty sure he was turning green. The air around him certainly was.

"Muskrats," Clygon shouted. "Hold your nose!"

Toby tried breathing through his mouth, but he could taste the musk smell! He started to gag, but soon, fresh mountain air filled his lungs.

By now, they were halfway down the mountain. Toby was on high alert, waiting for the next attack.

But it didn't come.

He sat up, held the sides of the centipede, took a deep breath, and relaxed. The ride was actually exhilarating. The view breathtaking.

"Uh oh!"

"Uh oh what?" Toby yelled.

"Hang on, Toby! Hang o—"

The centipedes stopped dead in their tracks, propelling Toby and Clygon over the front of them. They both landed hard on the ground and rolled for several moments down the mountain.

"Toby! Toby! Are you okay?"

Toby was a bit dazed and bruised. But all of his body parts were still intact.

"What was that?"

"We hit a Hava leeva pit at full speed."

"A javelina pit?"

"A Hava leeva pit. Havas are medium-sized bat-like, bird-like creatures who leave a lot of you-know-what behind."

"We hit a pile of…"

"Yup. And I don't know about you, but there's no way I'm going back to retrieve my centipede. We'll have to walk the rest of the way down. But it's not far now. See the river?"

Toby was starting to develop some nice bruises from the rock badgers and the fall from the centipede. But he was glad to be walking again. He felt a bit more in control.

Clygon pulled out a packet of jerky, offering some to Toby. They both still had some water left in their backpacks and, once refreshed, headed down toward the *River Glaedaan*.

"Do you have any idea where we're going or what we should do now?" Toby asked.

"Not…"

They both heard a sound. A pop.

They stood still, holding their breath. Listening.

But nothing.

They started walking again.

And again, a pop.

This time, Clygon kept walking, but he picked up the pace.

Then the air filled with the sound of pops. They couldn't see anything. They didn't feel anything. But the pops started boring into their ears. The louder the pops, the more agitated Toby and Clygon became.

"Cover your ears, Toby, and move as fast as you can."

It proved to be difficult running down a mountain holding their hands over their ears while growing increasingly agitated to the point of wanting to punch something.

"What is it?" Toby yelled out in anger.

"Weasels," Clygon shouted.

"Weasels?"

"Pop weasels. The males make that obnoxious popping sound during mating season."

"Ewwww…" Toby said.

Then something popped—metaphorically speaking—into Toby's mind.

"Don't tell me! Pop goes the weasel!"

He let out a groan.

Then, once again, all was quiet.

And that, it seemed, was the end of the adventure down the mountain. Now they stood at the banks of the *River Glaedaan,* a bit battered, tired, and still slightly agitated.

They both took off their shoes, rolled up their pant legs and stepped into the water. It was cold. But it felt so…

They heard swords being unsheathed.

"Don't move!"

13. Down by the River Side

They both froze. And then…

"Ha! Ha! Ha! Very funny, Judah."

Toby jumped up onto the riverbank and ran toward his river elf friend Judah to give him a hug, only to be tackled by Saaba.

Clygon climbed out of the river and joined them, giving Phoenix a fist bump while Judah tried to peel Saaba off of Toby.

"You two look like you've been through a war," Deckor said. "What happened?"

"You name it, it happened," Toby answered, finally able to climb back onto his feet. "Stalagmites… Stalactites… Rock badgers… Hava leeva pits…"

"Gross!" Phoenix said.

"But more important," Clygon jumped in, "or is it more importantly?"

They debated *important* vs *importantly* for a few moments when Judah finally made the timeout sign so that Clygon could get to what was so important.

"We found the giants!"

Deckor, Judah, and Phoenix looked at them in stunned silence.

"You couldn't lead with that?" Deckor asked. "Where? When? Give us the details."

"I was following a tip from the Christmas Giant," Clygon began.

"Trut Vater, as the giants call him—Truth Father," Toby added.

"They've been living in the middle of this mountain since they… well… since they disappeared. Can you believe it?" Clygon continued. "They've been here all along. They have an entire city built in there, along with huge metal forges and furnaces. Toby just showed up out of the blue, and we were befriended by some of the giants."

"But… why have they been hiding this whole time?" Phoenix asked.

Toby noticed he was wearing a Lamar Jackson jersey.

"They didn't want to get sucked into the divisiveness and hatred unleashed by the Chaos," Clygon explained. "So they withdrew. Yet all is not well in giant-land. Some of the giants want to re-engage with the world. But others support continued isolation. And that group made a pact with the trolls. The isolationists promised to give Plythar the Sword if the trolls would protect the mountain from outsiders."

"But… the giants don't have the Sword to give…"

Judah saw the look on Toby's face.

"They have the Sword, don't they?" Judah said.

"I… I had no choice. But.. but… it's useless anyway. It's missing a piece, and without that piece, the Sword will remain lifeless…"

"What is it, Clygon?" Deckor interrupted. "We know that look. You know something."

"Sorry, Toby," Clygon said with a big smile.

He reached into his backpack and pulled out a leather bag—and through the opening, Toby could see something glowing.

"Is that… the Sword? Did you switch bags? And you didn't think to tell me?"

"We needed you to be convincing for Lucas."

"So you don't trust my thespian skills? I'll have you know I played Rumpelstiltskin in first-grade summer school! And one of the workhouse boys in *Oliver!* at my church when I was in 5th grade."

"I'm sure you're an Academy Award winner, Toby, but not knowing how good you really are, we couldn't take the chance."

"Who's Lucas?" Judah asked.

Before Clygon could answer, Toby pointed to his backpack. Something was buzzing in it. He dug around until he found the source of the buzzing—the compass. Its needle was spinning wildly from the G to the O to the O to the D.

"It's trying to tell us something," Toby said.

And then the spinning stopped.

"What do the letters stand for?" Deckor asked, looking over Toby's shoulder at the compass.

"I don't know. Apparently we have to figure it out on our own this time around. The only clue we have is to *find the GOOD*."

"And what does that mean?" Phoenix asked.

Toby quickly explained the seven words embedded in the Sword and how the word GOOD—technically OOD—a tiny piece of the Sword, was missing.

"We think," Clygon said, "that the missing piece may be in the ground where Toby buried the Sword at my former stronghold."

They looked at each other for a moment as Phoenix, Judah, and Deckor tried to process what they had just heard.

"So… are you saying that we need to go to your former stronghold, sneak behind enemy lines, find the exact spot where Toby buried the Sword, find a piece of the Sword so tiny that you can hardly see it, sneak back through those same enemy lines to get to the giants, who are in some sort of civil war, so that they can put the Sword back together, and then take it back to *RiverHome* and put it in the stone before *Loach* loses all of its power?"

"Well… actually, we might have the resources to heal the Sword, but otherwise, that's a good summary of Toby's next Quest."

Toby felt a bolt of anxiety shoot through him at the thought of a new Quest.

"And don't forget, Phoenix," Judah said, "we have to figure out what G-O-O-D means for it all to work."

"You don't like to do things the easy way, do you Toby," Deckor laughed.

"Wait a minute," Toby said, putting the compass into his pocket while pushing back his growing anxiety, finally finding the thought that had been itching his brain. "What are you doing here? How did you find Saaba? This can't be a coincidence, can it? Or a kissit as Lucas says."

"I think it's kismet," Clygon added helpfully.

"Actually," Phoenix started, "now that we're here, it makes some sense. A few weeks ago, *Loach's* energy shifted. We could sense it in the earth. Clovor and I went to check it out, concerned that *Loach* was beginning to lose its strength. We know it's a backup for the Sword. We know it can't last much longer. When we approached it, we immediately noticed that the monument no longer said, *I.C.E. Call Toby Baxter*. It now reads, *I.C.E. Go North*. Not terribly helpful as there's a lot of north north of *RiverHome*." Phoenix laughed at his joke, if that's what it was.

"So the three of us set out last week, having no idea where we were going or why. We've been sticking pretty close to the river, and last night, we camped out not too far from here. We had decided to make our way up the mountain this morning when Saaba found us. He led us here… and here you are."

Saaba bowed. At least Toby thought he did.

"Did you get any information out of that troll Clovor dragged out of my hotel room?" Toby asked.

"None," answered Deckor. "He was too far down the food chain, so to speak, to have any information. But," Deckor thought for a moment, "he did say that if he failed in getting the Sword, Plythar would move on to plan B, and the B stands for Big. I wonder if that was Plythar's inside joke, knowing he would side with some of those giants."

"Hey! Is anybody else hungry?" Phoenix asked. "All this Quest talk makes me ravenous."

He sat down on a nearby log, pulled out a bag of ham and cheese sandwiches, passed them out, and the five of them, plus Saaba, ate quietly, trying to figure out their next move.

They heard the faint sounds of popping behind them up the mountain a ways.

"Not again," Toby sighed.

"It goes in cycles, Toby," Judah explained helpfully. "They call it—"

"No. Don't!"

"Pop-cycles!"

"And then it—"

"No. Really. Don't!"

"Re-cycles."

"Okay, Judah," Deckor said. "No more pop-corn for today!"

Phoenix high-fived his cousin. Toby rolled his eyes.

They cleaned up, washed up, and then sat down once again, this time to come up with a plan.

"Saaba," Phoenix said, "get the word out to Jerry and the gnomes, Oreea and the ogres, Blythar and his Resistance buddies, and to Donold, Clovor, and Mathilda back home. And of course our friends, the wolves. Here…"

Phoenix was writing on small pieces of paper with an oversized pen from *Disneyland* when he noticed Toby staring at him.

"What! I collect pens like I collect NFL jerseys." He proceeded to pull a handful of pens out of his backpack from *Al's Car Wash, Circle 8 Motel, IHop,* and others Toby didn't care to read.

"You can never have too many pens!" Deckor chimed in.

Phoenix attached the notes to Saaba's neck with pieces of twine. Saaba ran over to Toby, gave him a big wolf lick on his cheek, and took off downstream.

"Now… if you two are ready to go," Judah said, nodding to Toby and Clygon…

Suddenly, the earth shuddered underneath them. It was strong enough to knock Toby onto his butt. The shaking lasted fifteen seconds but felt like several minutes.

"Was that an earthquake? Do you have those here?" Toby asked, not able to hide the anxiety in his voice.

"That was no earthquake," Clygon said glumly. "I fear that something bad is happening in the middle of the mountain. We need to go. We need to find that missing Sword piece. Follow me. I know some secret back roads into the troll stronghold."

They quickly packed up their gear as they felt the ground shiver and shake once again. Toby looked up the mountain and prayed that Oliver, Evy, Harold, Pumpernickel, and the rest of the giants would be okay. He felt overwhelmed by the pressure of what was ahead.

"It's okay, Toby," Deckor whispered."

The ground shook again, knocking Deckor to his butt.

"Okay... maybe it's not oka—"

Just then, they heard what sounded like a boulder rolling down the mountain straight toward them. At once, they all looked up the mountain, searching for the cause of the sound. They could see trees moving back and forth like something was smashing its way through the middle of them.

The sound grew louder. They were about to jump out of the way of whatever it was that was rolling towards them when a giant broke through the trees. Followed by a second. Both of them had scrapes, bruises, and cuts on their faces and muscular arms. Both of them were holding swords.

The river elves stood frozen in shock, their mouths hanging open in the "I-can't-believe-I'm-actually-seeing-giants" expression.

"Oliver! Evy!" Toby shouted, running to them. "What's happening?"

"No... time... Toby," Oliver said, gasping for breath. "You and... your friends need to... run... Now! We'll hold them off... the best we can."

"Hold who off?" Clygon shouted.

"Go! Now! Find the GOOD!" Evy yelled. "Our fate is now in your hands, Toby and Clygon. Go!"

Toby felt a hand grabbing his arm. It was Judah, now apparently recovered from his initial shock.

Just as Toby was turning to run, he saw them… dozens of giants and trolls, weapons drawn, hurtling their way down the mountain, with only Oliver and Evy to stop them.

"We can't leave them," Toby yelled as he tried to pull free from Judah. "They don't stand a chance."

Clygon grabbed him.

"Toby! The only chance they have is for you to find the GOOD and heal the Sword. Let's go! They're counting on you."

As they ran along the river away from the battle and toward the trolls' stronghold, Toby could hear the clanging of swords and the cries of pain.

Anger mixed with despair filled him.

He let out a scream.

Something behind him exploded.

And then everything went dark.

14. Hitting the Brakes

"Woooo hoooo…"

Sid's voice was up ahead of him.

The cool mist of the fog, or perhaps it was a cloud, hit his face, jarring him into the moment.

How did I get back here?

"I can't see Toby," Toby's mom cried out. "Toby, are you in front of us or behind us, dear?"

Her voice came from up ahead.

Wasn't she behind me a moment ago?

"I think I'm… behind you… Mom…" Toby yelled out into the cloud. "And don't call me dear in public," he muttered.

The crabby Toby was back.

No. That wasn't it. A sense of foreboding filled him. Something very bad had just happened.

Oliver! Evy! The mountain!

He hit the brakes. Too hard. The bike slid… he hit the ground… hard…

Toby…

The voice came from somewhere far away…

Toby, old boy. Are you okay?

Toby opened his eyes to see the big smiling face of Author. He was wearing a fluorescent green cycling helmet, sports sunglasses, and a bicycle jersey with a brightly colored beach pattern with *Author's Write* imprinted on it. *Does that count as a homonym?*

There he is, Author said, helping Toby sit up.

"What happened?"

You hit the brakes a bit too hard, the bike skidded, and you hit the ground too hard, I'm afraid. Nothing seems to be broken, but your shoulder is going to feel it for a while. Good thing you had your helmet on.

Author noticed Toby looking above his head.

Guess you knocked yourself right out of the story, Author laughed.

"Toby? Toby?"

"Mom?"

Author looked over his shoulder toward the voice.

Toby felt his eyes closing…

Toby…

Again the voice came from far away…

Toby…

"Toby! Toby! Wake up! There you go. You're okay. Here. Let me help you."

Toby struggled to sit up. His shoulder hurt. His elbow hurt. His ribs hurt. His whole body hurt.

"Drink this."

A cup was brought to his lips.

The river elf drink.

How did I get back here?

The drink immediately energized him and seemed to numb the pain.

"What happened?"

He looked around. It was dark. A small fire burned off to his right. The river flowed next to him on his left. The sky was bright, filled with stars. Four faces stood inches... *Do faces stand?...* from his face, worry etched in all of them. *Etched?* Phoenix. Judah. Deckor. Clygon.

"Oliver! Evy!" Toby suddenly remembered what had just happened.

"Have another sip of this," Clygon said, pouring more of the river elf elixir into Toby's mouth.

"How long have I been out?"

"You've been missing for over twenty-four hours," Judah said, not able to hide his concern and relief.

Either it was too dark to see the words above their heads, or Toby was back into the story. Probably the second option.

"Missing? Twenty-four hours? But I was only gone for a minute…"

"Were you back home?" Deckor asked.

"Back on the bike in Hawaii. Last thing I remember was a huge explosion. Did something happen on the mountain? To the giants?"

"We have no idea," Phoenix said. "As we were running from the mountain, you let out a huge scream. And just like the time you screamed when you planted the Sword at Clygon's stronghold, something exploded, and you disappeared. You knocked all of us out for several minutes, and when we came to, you were gone. We've spent hours looking for you, and fortunately, we finally found you here. About three miles south of where we were."

"Three miles? In a minute? Wow… Take that Flash!" Toby tried to laugh, but it hurt his ribs. "I guess I need to time my screams better."

A loud boom sounded from the mountain, now several miles away.

"We've been hearing those off and on," Judah said.

Toby ached to know what had happened to Oliver and Evy. He also felt a new surge of energy.

"Is it night or early morning?" he asked. "We need to get going."

"It's near midnight. If you're up for it, we're ready to go. From now on, it will be best for us to travel under the cover of darkness. We're about two days away from the stronghold. Perhaps three, depending on what we encounter along the way," Clygon said ominously.

Toby stood up hesitantly. His right shoulder hurt. A lot. Deckor handed him some jerky. Toby wolfed it down in three bites and washed it down with more elven drink. He felt about as good as he was going to feel.

"Okay. Let's go."

For the next several hours, they followed Clygon, staying close to the riverbank. Feeling discombobulated—*still a great word!*—Toby concentrated on putting one foot in front of the other to keep from stumbling or tripping. The night air was cool, which helped keep him awake. But the numbing effect of the river elf elixir was wearing off, and he was starting to feel sore all over his body. At least he wasn't concussed. No headache. No fuzziness. He obviously landed on his right shoulder and elbow. That's where the pain was most intense.

Deckor sensed Toby slowing, so he called for a break.

Being near the river, they all removed their shoes and put their feet in the water. It felt like icicles. Toby immediately pulled his feet out and then re-immersed them a few times to get them used to the cold. It helped revive him.

They ate some jerky and drank some elixir in the quietness of the pre-dawn morning. The sounds of nature—crickets, bird calls, animals scurrying through the grass—helped ease some of the disease Toby was starting to feel once again. The Quest before them was impossible. He knew it. His friends knew it.

Before he talked himself into total despair, he stood up, put on his shoes, and said, "We have a world to save. Let's get moving."

Clygon, Judah, Deckor, and Phoenix looked at him.

And then broke out laughing.

Toby was flummoxed. *Flummoxed? I really need a notebook to jot down all of these words.*

"What's so funny?" he asked.

"It's... not you... it's just... that..." Deckor said, trying to contain himself. "Well... actually... it is you. You looked so serious. And really, this whole Quest is ridiculous. What else is there to do but laugh about it and do as you say—get moving."

They packed up their gear and headed back downstream.

"I still don't know what was so funny," Toby muttered.

"No offense, Toby," Judah said. "We were releasing nervous energy. The task ahead of us is... well... not an easy one, to say the least. We're all a bit scared..."

"You? You're scared?"

"Of course we are, Toby," Phoenix said. "But what's important right now—"

"Shhh!" Clygon turned to them with his finger to his lips.

They all stopped.

"I hate to interrupt your big Quest motivational talk, Phoenix," Clygon whispered. "But…"

He pointed up ahead and to his right.

The glow of a fire bounced off of the trees.

"Trolls?" Deckor whispered.

"Probably," Clygon answered. "I'm guessing they're an outpost as a first line of defense to protect the mountain."

"So… Plythar's trolls," Phoenix said, stating the obvious.

Clygon hunched down, motioning for the others to do the same.

"We're going to head east, away from the river. We'll have to take a slight detour to make sure we're well clear of the trolls. But we need to get some rest. It's just about sunup. About two miles from here is an old cave I found when I was a kid…"

Clygon paused. He seemed to choke back a sob.

"I had just lost my parents…"

Another pause.

"Anyway, I did a lot of wandering on my own. It's a place no one else knows about. It's also why I know some ways into the stronghold no one else is aware of. It will take us about forty-five minutes. Go quietly."

Toby felt like he was holding his breath for those forty-five minutes. Every crack of a twig under his feet sounded like a loud crash of thunder. But Clygon was right. They didn't see any signs of trolls and made it safely to the cave.

Without saying anything, they laid out their sleeping bags, and within moments, all of them were asleep—except for the big, yellow eyes watching them from the corner.

15. Para-dies

The bright sunlight woke him up.

Wait. We're in a cave!

He sat up.

Clygon, Judah, Phoenix, and Deckor were fast asleep.

In the cave.

The sunlight was coming from inside of the cave!

That doesn't make sense.

He slowly crawled out of his sleeping bag so as not to wake the others. The scent of some sort of flower wafted... *stop with the wafting...* over him. He took a few steps deeper into the cave—deeper into the sunlight, where a wall was supposed to be—and soon found himself in the middle of a lush garden. Huge ferns, trees, and bushes with the sunlight breaking through them filled the sky above. It was the largest, most beautiful garden he had ever seen. Somewhere off in the distance, he heard a waterfall. Something about the place filled him with a sense of deep calm.

Up ahead, he heard a giggle. A female giggle. He looked behind him and saw that the others were still asleep. Then he heard the giggle again, and when he turned toward the sound...

"Rainie?"

Before him stood a girl about his age. Long blonde hair. A small mole just above her lip to the right of her nose. She was about five feet, four inches tall. She wore a tie-dyed shirt with the Hawaiian Islands on the left shoulder—but the islands were upside down—a pair of black shorts, and blue Crocs.

Rainie? She looks like Rainie... not the giant Rainie I just met but the Rainie from school. Except... except for the eyes. Rainie has cat-like eyes. Mesmerizing. Mysterious. Beauti—

Get a grip, Toby.

This girl had yellow eyes with weird pupils. They seemed to have a small slit in them. They looked like the eyes of a... snake! And they stared right through him.

"Hellooo Toby," she said.

"Who are you? Where am I?" Toby asked. She seemed harmless and friendly enough.

"My name is Sopha."

She had a very pleasing, soothing voice.

"Sofa? Like in a couch?"

"No, silly Toby. Sopha. As in wisdom."

Something is off.

"Don't you mean Sophia?" Toby said, dreamily. "My Aunt's name is Sophia, and she's always reminding me that her name means wisdom so I should always listen to her. I think you're a letter short of wisdom." He hoped he had not caused offense.

Sopha giggled. But the giggle seemed a bit darker than before.

"I'm here to help you find the good. That's a part of your quest, correct? To find the good? That's what I'm here for."

That got Toby's attention.

"How did you know…"

"All knowledge, including goodness, is built on wisdom, Toby," she continued. "Hence my name: Sopha. Wisdom."

"Um… but shouldn't it be Sophia?"

"That's what makes me the perfect guide in helping you find the good. Check your compass. It should be coming to life right about now."

Toby pulled the compass out from his pocket. It was dead. He showed it to Sopha.

"Hmmm… That's odd. Oh well. It should spring to life once I show you the good."

Toby.

It was the voice of his Grandpa Baxter. The Christmas Giant.

Toby. Listen to your heart. Something isn't right.

"This is my home, by the way," she continued on, moving her arm to encompass the garden. "Para-dies."

"Paradise?"

"Sure. If that works for you. You say ta-may-toe. I say ta-maa-toe."

"Huh?"

"Anyway, you're my guest, Toby. So let's stop listening to those voices in your head, shall we? Come with me."

How did she know about the voice in my head? But her voice was so soothing. The garden so calming. He couldn't help himself. He followed her deeper into Para-dies.

She started humming. The melody made him feel a bit woozy... tired... foggy-brained. *Foggy-brained?*

She turned to look at him.

Toby stopped. For just a moment, he thought her face had become that of a snake.

"What is it, Toby?" she purred.

Toby shook his head.

"Nothing. I'm tired. I'm seeing things."

The voice of his grandpa tried to warn him. *Trust your heart, Tob—*

"We're just about there, Toby. You see that great big tree in the middle of the garden? The one with the huge apples growing on it?"

Toby began to drool. The apples were calling to him. Luring him with the promise of sweet goodness. And he was hungry.

She led him up to the tree.

"This is the source of the good. Take one," she said, pointing to the apples.

"Really?"

She nodded yes.

He reached out for the biggest apple his hand could grab. It felt pleasing to the touch. It felt… well… good. It felt right.

"… the thing about good, Toby," Sopha's voice eased back into his mind, "is that it requires some compromises…"

"Compromises?" he asked as he pulled the apple off of the branch.

Toby! The Christmas Giant whispered with more urgency.

"For example," she continued, "if you truly want to be good, you need to put yourself above others."

"But that's not what the Christmas Giant—"

"He's dead!" she hissed, her snake face reappearing.

Toby took a step back. Something was definitely off. He tried to turn around, but Sopha touched his arm. Her touch was so soft. So reassuring.

"Think about it, Toby. If you always put others first, you're going to wear yourself out. You won't have anything left to give them. You must develop tough skin. You have to…"

She paused, taking a moment to think.

He eyeballed the apple in his hand. His mouth watered.

Toby...

His grandpa's voice was getting softer, harder to hear.

"The g in good stands for grab..." Sopha said, apparently having wrapped up her moment to think.

"Grab? Grab what?"

"Life, Toby. What is it you want out of life? What are the deep desires of your heart? Focus on you, Toby. To be good, you need to be #1..."

"But... A HERO..." he began to explain.

"Toby, when you're on an airplane, and the flight attendant talks about what to do should there be a sudden drop in the air cabin pressure and the oxygen masks drop down, what is the first thing the attendant instructs a parent traveling with a child to do?"

"Um... put on a mask first and then..."

"That's right. You need to grab that oxygen mask first, Toby. You're no good if you can't breathe!"

"I guess that makes sense... but you still need to put the mask on the..."

"Or how about the thingy you learn in your church..."

When she said the word church, she looked like she'd just swallowed a raw piece of dead fish.

"Thingy?"

"You need to love yourself before you can even begin to think about your neighbor." She said this was some malice in her eyes.

"That's not actually quite right, and again—"

"Toby, if you're going to be good, you have to put your needs and wants ahead of those of everyone else. You need to grab what you want before others do."

Toby… she's twisting…

"The o in good is for optimization."

"Opti-what?"

"Optimization. Optimize your brand, Toby."

"My brand?"

"Yes. You need to rise above the crowd. Make a name for yourself. When people hear 'Toby Baxter', you want them to immediately think about you! What you stand for! What makes you you in such a way that they want to be like you… to follow you… to do whatever you do or buy whatever you're selling. #TobyBaxter. Sounds good, doesn't it?"

It did sound good.

"The second o stands for obliterate. Obliterate the competition, Toby. You need to be ruthless. How else are you going to stand up to Plythar and the trolls? Or Derrick, for that matter. You can't do it by being nice, Toby."

"That… does… make sense."

Toby… please… listen… to…

"Finally, the d stands for dominate. Own yourself, Toby. Stand tall. Let them see that you don't need anyone else. You are self-sufficient. You are *The* Toby Baxter."

She paused.

"Say it, Toby. Say—I am *The* Toby Baxter!"

"I am the Toby Baxter!"

"Say it again, with more confidence."

"I am *The* Toby Baxter!"

"Your compass must be on fire!"

It wasn't. It was still dead.

But the apple in his hand had started to glow. Fire-red.

It was also burning his hand. The pain was moving up his arm.

Sopha noticed and gave him a smile.

"I know it hurts, Toby, but hold onto it just a bit longer. It's forging the power of good into you."

"I'm not sure…" The pain had caused tears to leak out of his eyes.

She closed her soft, warm hand over his to make sure he didn't let go of the apple.

"Remember when that christmas giant friend of yours…" she spit out the words, "said in your second book…"

"My second book?"

"…that a part of being wise is to be resilient? Well… consider this an exercise in building resilience. Hold on, Toby! This will only make you stronger."

The apple-glow grew brighter, the burning deeper, more painful…

"Now, Toby, take a big bite. The bigger the bite, the deeper the good will go into your soul. Take… a… bite… Toby, and join me…"

"Join you," Toby said in a daze.

Sopha guided his hand to his mouth. He could see his image in the apple. But what he saw horrified him. His face was distorted… disfigured… terrifying…

"Toby!" It sounded like Judah.

Sopha turned and hissed. Then she shrieked. The most horrific, frightening shriek Toby had ever heard. Worse than Clygon's battle cries back when Clygon was his enemy. It twisted his stomach into knots.

A giant snakehead fell at his feet, its mouth still moving, as if trying to dig its big fangs into him. Some sort of oozy stuff covered the front of him. The apple lay at his feet, shriveled and purple.

He fell backwards.

Clygon caught him.

He was back in the cave.

Judah was forcing the elven elixir into his mouth. Deckor was putting something on his burned hand, an ointment of some sort. It stung to the point that he felt nauseous. He watched as Phoenix stuck a sword through the serpent's head, making sure it was really dead. *Hey, that rhymed.*

Through a haze, he heard Clygon say, "He needs a Healer. Or a Songstress. Probably both. Soon. The poison is already moving up his arm."

Toby looked down and saw that his arm was slowly turning purple. The pain was intense.

But so was something else.

Anger.

Defiance.

"Let me go!" he yelled. "Do you know who I am? I am *The Toby Baxter!*"

The force of his voice threw them all backwards.

Toby struggled to his feet.

"This is my quest! This is my chance to make a name for myself. From now on, we do things my way or—"

"Do something!" Judah yelled. "We're losing him!"

Toby saw the river elves surrounding him, ready to pounce.

Be ruthless, Toby! Dominate! Stay on brand, Toby! It's the only way to be good.

Sopha's voice seemed to speak to him from the pain in his arm.

He took a step toward Judah.

But it was too late.

"Sorry, Toby. You leave me no choice," Clygon whispered from behind him.

Clygon's arm wrapped itself around Toby's neck while the other arm grabbed Toby's head and gently moved it forward.

"Not the sleeper-hold…"

16. Snake Bit

*C*eltic humming.

Toby...

"Mathilda?"

Yes, Toby. I'm here. It's going to be okay.

"What's going to be okay? What happ..."

Images of a girl... an apple tree... a snake head...

"My arm hurts. It's like something is squeezing the life out of it."

Keep listening to the sound of my voice, Toby. Let the humming relax you. I'm going to help with the pain.

More images... a garden... yellow eyes...

Toby. Your arm has been infected. We have to stop the poison. The Healer is out looking for Tyde.

"Tied as in an even score? Tied as in your hands bound together? Tide as in the rising and falling of the ocean based on the sun and the moon? Or Tide as in the detergent?"

English grammar and spelling!

He sensed Mathilda sigh and shake her head.

No. This is Tyde. T-Y-D-E. It's a derivative of the Bleech bush. It's the only thing that can remove the stain you've... um... well... sustained... so to speak.

Toby attempted a smile.

"Where am I?"

You're in a dream state, Toby. I'm speaking to your subconscious. I'm trying to bring some relief and healing to your memory while the Healer looks for the Tyde.

"Is this something like what Sid went through when he was here? He told me that your grandma helped him after he saw some bad stuff when he grabbed the hilt of *Loach*."

Yes, exactly. We didn't know it at the time but Grandma was a Songstress, an assistant to the Healers. Before she passed away…

"Wait… Grandma passed away? When? How?"

The humming took on a tone of grief and loss.

She died three of our years ago, Toby. She had become very weak. And she so missed Grandpa. One day she called Donold into her bedroom and said, 'I can't do this anymore.' She sat down in her chair, closed her eyes, and went to join our Elven ancestors, including Grandpa. We didn't get a chance to say goodbye.

Toby felt himself weeping, even though he was apparently in a dream.

"I'm so very, very sorry, Mathilda. She was such a… a… good woman."

The tone of the humming changed again. A bit brighter.

Toby... what do you think made her good?

A stab of pain seared through his arm. It was getting closer to his shoulder.

Stay with me, Toby. Concentrate. What made her a good woman?

"She was... she was a very generous person."

Something buzzed in his pocket. *The compass? Can a compass buzz when you're in a dream?*

What do you mean? Mathilda asked.

"Well... she was always giving of herself to others. If someone needed something, she didn't hesitate to help out. She put others ahead of herself."

Did that make her weak, Toby?

"Weak?" Toby laughed. "She was one of the strongest..."

A memory stirred.

If you're always going to put others first, you'll wear yourself out.... You can't win by being nice...

Someone had just told him that. That girl... with the snake eyes...

Grab! Optimize! Obliterate! Dominate!

The humming grew louder, trying to drown out his thoughts, as if doing battle with an unseen force.

Sopha! The girl... in the garden... with the apple...

His hand was burning.

You are THE Toby Baxter! Say it with me...

Mathilda's humming took on a new sense of urgency.

Grab! Optimize! Obliterate! Dominate!

His arm was screaming at him.

You want to be good, don't you Toby? Join me... join m...

Now Mathilda was singing. Words Toby didn't understand. Ancient elven words. *A prayer perhaps?*

This is not over...

But then it was.

Mathilda's humming had won out.

Toby relaxed. And felt embarrassed.

"I'm sorry, Mathilda. I don't know where that came from. Something's wrong with me."

It's going to take some time to minimize the damage from the stain, Toby. In the meantime, remember Grandma and what you just said about her. It will help lead you to the GOOD when the time comes.

The humming quieted down, as if distracted.

Finally! The Healer is here. Go to sleep, Toby. I'll see you soon.

"His eyes are opening!"

The voice belonged to Clygon.

But the first face he saw was Mathilda's. She looked exhausted. *Did I do that to her?* She threw her arms around him and buried her head in his shoulder, weeping.

Then Judah's face came into view.

"Welcome back, Toby!"

Toby could hear the relief in his voice.

"Okay, Mathilda, give him some space. Let me take a look at his arm."

Mathilda moved, and the Healer sat down beside him.

"How are you feeling, Toby? How is the arm? Can you move it?"

Toby brought his right wrist up to his right shoulder. It felt stiff. Sore. But it was much better. He noticed that it was wrapped in light green leaves. They smelled a bit of laundry detergent.

"Tyde?" he asked.

The Healer nodded. "We'll keep them on for at least the next twenty-four hours, Toby. We need to get as much of that stuff out of you as possible. The color is looking much better."

Toby sat up.

Phoenix brought him some jerky.

"I'm guessing you're hungry."

"Starving. Thanks, Phoenix."

After a few bites, he asked, "What happened?"

Deckor started to hum. A story was coming…

"We had camped out in a cave. Our intent was to sleep through the day and travel by night. Clygon was the first to notice it. A presence. Something evil. You weren't in your sleeping bag. Next to it was the shed skin of a huge snake."

"Sopha!" Clygon took over the story. "The temptress. Her sole job is to disfigure us. To make us less than who we are. She does that by telling us just enough truth to lure us into her trap and then… Bam! She snaps it shut, and we find ourselves living life on the basis of her lies."

"She had you caught in a vision. I'm guessing Para-dies?" Deckor asked.

"I thought she said Paradise," Toby said.

"Hardly. What we saw was a big snake, its head hanging over you, holding you in a trance. Your hand went out as if grabbing something…"

"An apple." Toby said.

"And then you started to shake," Phoenix jumped in, "as if you were in deep pain. We saw your arm starting to turn purple, and we knew she had poisoned you. Clygon lopped off her head... which was pretty darn cool by the way."

"So... there was no garden? No apple? No rather attractive girl who looked a lot like my... um... like a girl I once knew?"

"No. It was all an illusion."

"She told me she was going to lead me to the good."

"But it wasn't GOOD, was it?" Clygon smirked.

They all fell silent.

"How did Mathilda and the Healer get here? We were halfway to the trolls' stronghold."

Judah held up what looked like a whistle. "I sent a message to our flying dragon friend, Ruphas. He flew them here. And just in time, too. We were pretty sure we'd lost you."

"Saaba had already alerted us to head to the trolls' stronghold," Mathilda said, looking down at the wolf, now sound asleep. "He ran for hours without a break to get to us. Clovor and Donold are on their way now with some of our elite soldiers."

"But... surely the trolls would see a flying dragon and try to find where it landed?"

"It was nighttime, so we're hopeful that they didn't see him," Mathilda said. "But we can't be sure."

More silence as they let Toby take in what had happened.

"Is… is… Sopha dead?"

"No, Toby, she's not dead." This time, it was the Healer. "Temporarily defeated. She's a primeval force. From time before time. She roams the land, tempting people with her lies. Distorting goodness. Twisting wisdom. She was behind the Chaos."

The Healer closed his eyes and continued:

For still our ancient foe

Doth seek to work us woe

Her craft and power are great

And armed with cruel hate.

Toby had heard those words before, or something similar to them, but he couldn't quite work out where.

"But," Clygon said, "at least for today, Para-dies lost. And you lived to tell about it."

Deckor's humming stopped.

"Toby, if you're up for it, we really need to take advantage of the darkness and get moving. We've already lost a day…"

"Seriously, Clygon?" Mathilda chided.

"I'm okay. Really," Toby said, appreciating the word chided. "You're right. We should go."

They quickly packed up their gear while the Healer checked the Tyde on Toby's arm.

"Are you coming with us?" he asked Mathilda and the Healer.

"Wouldn't miss it, Toby! And since you can't keep yourself from getting into trouble, probably best we do," Mathilda answered.

With that, they stepped into the night.

The eyes of the dead snake head snapped open.

Toby's arm twitched.

You are The Toby Baxter, a voice hissed.

17. Stained

It rained the entire night. The kind of unrelenting rain that seeps into your clothes, your skin, your soul, and your mood. And Toby's mood was foul. Again. They all walked with their heads down, their hooded cloaks having given up the battle to keep them dry hours ago. Poor Saaba looked like a walking wool rug.

They stopped for a break from time to time to eat soggy jerky and take their nature breaks in the pouring rain.

The Healer seemed pleased with the progress on Toby's arm, but Toby could feel the lingering effects of whatever it was Sopha had done to him. From time to time, his arm would twitch, sending pain from his fingers to his shoulder. And with it, anger. And a deep sense of injustice—the injustice of him, *The* Toby Baxter, having to travel under the cover of darkness and in the pouring rain. *Don't they know who I am?*

And then he felt sick about thinking that way.

Every now and then he could sense Mathilda looking at him. He refused to meet her eyes, although, admittedly, it was impossible to see her eyes through the dark rain. Instead, he focused on how he might brand himself on social media. Perhaps *@TobyBaxter*. Or better yet, *@THETobyBaxter*. Yes. Much better…

He shook his head. This was not who…

Selfies! He needed some selfies to post on social media. Wouldn't it be cool if his friends saw him riding on Ruphas? Or holding the Sword? He could become *The Boy of the Quest*. Or perhaps *Toby of the Sword*. Or *Toby the Dragon Flyer*. Needs some work. *This branding thing is not easy.*

And imagine what he might do to the school bully, Derrick! He could obliterate him through a series of tweets—or whatever they're called now—or posts or through the collective energy of his multitude of followers. To see Derrick sniveling and Toby's followers cheering him on as he dealt one emotional body blow after another to his arch nemesis…

He wanted to throw up.

"Toby?"

It was Mathilda.

"Are you okay?"

"I'm fine," he muttered.

He heard a deep, creepy laugh radiating from his arm.

"Really?" Mathilda asked.

He opened his mouth, then closed it. Then opened it again:

"Something's wrong," he said before he could change his mind. "I have these thoughts… awful thoughts… fighting inside of me."

"That's the stain talking, Toby. We're doing what we can to diminish its effects. In the meantime, don't fight it alone. We're here for you, Toby. We will get you through this."

She put out her arm to stop him. She pulled back the hood on her head. Then, standing on the tips of her toes, she did the same with Toby's hood. Their heads were already soaked, but the cool air brought Toby back into the present.

Still on her toes, she looked him in the eyes, more like looked up into his eyes.

She smiled.

"I still see you in there, Toby!"

She pulled his hood back over his head, which in that short time had filled with rain water and doused him down his back.

He shivered.

"What do you think of *#TeamToby* T-shirts?" he asked.

Mathilda's eyebrows shot up, which was quite the trick because, like Mr Spock's eyebrows, they were already up.

"Just kidding!" he said. *Although…*

The two of them ran to catch up to the group who had stopped by an old, abandoned stone hut.

Clygon was just climbing out of it.

"It's dry. It's fairly roomy. And it's probably our best chance to dry out and get some sleep."

As they settled in, the Healer examined Toby's arm. It now looked more pale yellow than dark purple. He was also able to move it more freely. The Healer applied a fresh bandage of Tyde leaves and gave Toby a small sip of some sort of awful-tasting herb.

"Yuck. What was that?"

"It works like an antibiotic. I'm hoping it will bring some healing from the inside to supplement the Tyde on the outside. You're making good progress, Toby. But be patient. Sopha's bite leaves its mark."

He saw the concern in Toby's eyes.

"Look at this, Toby."

The Healer rolled up the sleeve on his left arm, revealing a yellow-purple blotch.

"Is that…"

"Yes. We've all been stained by Sopha's lies, Toby. Every one of us here. We all struggle with wanting to do the right thing and choosing not to, or not wanting to do the wrong thing and doing it anyway. But you don't have to listen to her voice. She doesn't have to have the final word in your life."

Those were the last words Toby heard. Exhausted from his encounter with Sopha, the stain, and the long walk through the pouring rain, he fell asleep while the rest of the group set up camp in the stone hut.

He had strange dreams. Vivid dreams. Snake eyes… apples… holding the Sword in his hands as its energy flowed out of him, causing people to bow before him, cowering in fear… his river elf friends pleading with him to put the Sword down… Derrick in tears as Toby and his friends insulted and teased him… His mom and dad worried about how angry and rebellious he had become… Sid walking away from him, no longer willing to be his friend… Looking at himself in a mirror and seeing his face twisted in anger and then lit up with power and then broken with sadness... *Toby*...The voice of his Grandpa Baxter... *Toby*...The Christmas Giant stood in front of him, that big, genuine, 'glad-to-see-you' smile on his face. He reached out, putting his hand on Toby's forehead, and whispered some words...

He woke with a start. *Woke with a start? What does that even mean?*

Even though it was cold from the damp, he was soaked from sweating. His mouth was dry. He had a headache and felt weak.

And someone's hand was on his forehead. It was the Healer. Next to the Healer sat Mathilda, softly humming a Celtic tune that seeped into his soul and calmed him.

"You're through the worst of it now, Toby," the Healer said with a smile. "You've had quite a night. You spiked a fever soon after you fell asleep. It broke an hour ago, thankfully."

Toby could sense the others moving about the small hut.

"How long have I been sleeping?"

"About fourteen hours, sleepy head. Get some food in you. We need to get moving," Clygon said.

The Healer removed the Tyde leaves from Toby's arm. His arm was almost back to normal. A very slight bruising, hardly noticeable, still colored it.

"You saw the Christmas Giant, didn't you, Toby," Mathilda whispered. "In your dream."

"How did you know that?"

"I saw him, too. I was singing over you at the moment he touched your head. That's when the fever broke."

She smiled, then stood up and headed over to talk with Phoenix. Deckor appeared and gave Toby some food and drink.

"We'll take it easy on you, Toby. You've had a rough few days. Clygon says we should be to the stronghold by the morning. Then we'll find a place to sleep, and then… Toby magic time. You find the GOOD and save the world. Simple."

"Here," Clygon said, throwing him some clothes. "Put these on. They're dry. At least they are now. It's still pouring outside."

"Awesome!"

Clygon turned and then turned back to Toby. He squatted down and looked him in the eyes. He was getting a lot of looks in the eyes as of late.

"You look like yourself again, Toby. It's good to have you back."

Deckor offered Toby a hand up. Toby headed to a somewhat private area and changed out of his rain-and-sweat-soaked clothes into dry ones: a light leather shirt, leather pants—both dark green—thick socks, boots, and a heavy hooded leather cloak. He made sure to transfer the compass to his dry pants pocket.

He threw his backpack on and headed to the door, but not before catching a whiff of Christmas.

18. Good Thinking?

The rain continued to pummel them, making their progress slow as they tried to maneuver their way around or through increasingly large pools of water or mud. It was also tough to discern troll outposts. The rain, combined with the darkness of night, made it hard to see more than a foot or so ahead, and impossible to hear anything but the rain pelting their hoods.

But Clygon knew the area well. They stayed as close as possible to each other, trusting Clygon to get them to wherever they were going. At one point, he stopped. His head moved to the right and then to the left. Then he turned, nodded to the rain-soaked group, and headed northwest.

Several times, Toby tripped on exposed tree roots or bumped his head on low-hanging branches. He found he was moving more and more slowly. Occasionally, they would stop so that Toby could refuel with jerky and the elven drink.

"Not far now, Toby," Clygon said. "Another forty-five minutes and we'll find somewhere warm and dry."

It seemed a long forty-five minutes. An uneasy feeling slowly crept into his heart and soul, making his skin crawl. *Does skin crawl?*

"Wake up, Toby!"

Apparently, Toby had nodded off while walking, *which is kind of cool when you think about it,* dreaming of something creepy crawly. *Crawling skin, perhaps?*

Judah and Deckor walked on each side of him to keep him from stumbling or falling asleep on his feet.

Toby's mind was numb. Each step seemed to take minutes. He was shivering from the cold. Just as he was about to scream out in frustration, they stopped.

"We're here," Clygon said. "Troll village is about a mile north of us."

Here meant another abandoned stone hut.

"I used to come here to get away from…" Clygon started.

Toby remembered the vision he had seen of Clygon on his last *RiverHome* Quest. Clygon had been bullied. Not unlike Toby had been bullied by Derrick.

The place was dry. And remarkably warm. They didn't dare risk a fire, so it was jerky yet again.

"We'll sleep through the daylight. We'll need to take turns keeping watch. I don't think much will happen with this rain, but still…" Clygon let the thought hang.

Judah and Mathilda volunteered for the first watch while the rest of them set up a makeshift camp inside the hut. The Healer checked on Toby's arm and seemed pleased, but did advise Toby to get some sleep. His body had experienced too much trauma in too short a period of time.

Toby needed no convincing. And in no time, he was sound asleep. This time without any bad dreams.

He woke up feeling better than he had in days. He climbed out of his sleeping bag and gently walked over a sleeping Deckor and Judah. Just outside the door sat Clygon, staring off toward the troll stronghold.

"I haven't been home in thirteen years," he said, sensing Toby's presence. "It's an odd experience to have grown up there," he nodded in the direction of the stronghold, "then become a baby again, and yet remember so many things. And most of them, from this perspective, not very pleasant."

He continued to stare off toward home.

"What's the plan?" Toby asked.

Dusk was approaching. The rain had stopped, but the skies were still cloudy.

"In a few hours, once everyone has rested up, we'll make our way to the meeting grounds where you planted the Sword. The scene is burned into my soul, so I'm pretty sure I know exactly where to look for the GOOD. Let's hope it's there."

"And if it isn't?" Toby asked.

Mathilda quietly slipped down next to Toby.

"I had an insight about that," she said. "What if…"

They heard a loud horn off in the distance.

Clygon jumped to his feet.

"That's a battle horn. The trolls are being called to battle."

"Battle? Against who?" Toby asked, jumping to his feet.

"Against whom…" Mathilda corrected.

They were joined by Deckor, Judah, Phoenix, and the Healer.

"I don't think we have the luxury of finding out," Clygon said. "We need to get in and out of the stronghold as quickly and quietly as we can before whatever is happening has time to happen."

He ran into the hut, as did the rest of them, to pack their gear.

Geared up, they headed into the heart of troll-land. Toby could sense the anxiety level rising in all of them. They were on high-alert. The battle horn had sounded one more time, but they had seen nothing to indicate that an attack was about to break out near them.

After about thirty minutes of walking through the muddy forest, Clygon stopped and gathered the group around him.

"Just beyond that rise…" Clygon pointed.

"Is the stronghold!" Phoenix said.

Mathilda let out a soft groan and started to shake uncontrollably.

Toby thought back to that dark night—*just six months ago my time? Decades ago for my river elf friends? A timey wimey thing!* He could still see it vividly in his mind. He was standing on the field in front of Clygon and the grandstands filled with trolls. He watched as two trolls unfurled a blanket in front of him, dropping its contents—Mathilda—onto the ground, almost lifeless. No one but Mathilda knew of the horrors she had suffered at the hands of Clygon in the cells of the stronghold.

Judah threw his arms around her and held her tight, seemingly trying to absorb her pain.

Clygon stepped toward her, but she flinched. He put his hands up as if to say, 'I mean you no harm.' He touched her forearm. She tried to pull it away, but he held it. And he held her eyes. Judah let go of her and walked away.

Clygon sat down with Mathilda next to him. He began to speak to her, quietly, but urgently. Mathilda just as quietly began to weep.

Judah, Phoenix, Deckor, and the Healer surrounded them and began a quiet, low hum. Toby stood just outside the circle, watching.

Suddenly, and surprisingly, Clygon began to weep. His shoulders shook up and down. Now it was Mathilda hanging onto his arm.

"How? You can't. Don't! I don't deserve it."

"I must, Clygon. I have to let it go for my sake. And for yours. I can't live in this fear anymore. I can't live with the... the... the pain."

She leaned toward him and whispered in his ear. Softly. But Toby heard it.

"I forgive you, Clygon."

Toby turned away, but Phoenix waved him over, and he joined the circle. He let the music seep into his soul. While it was meant for Clygon and Mathilda, the humming filled him with hope.

After several minutes, the group fell silent.

Clygon stood up and helped Mathilda to her feet.

Then he looked each one of them in the eyes, holding eye contact for a few moments. First Deckor... then Judah... then Phoenix... followed by the Healer... then Saaba... and lastly, Toby. Clygon said nothing. He simply held their eyes until each of them nodded.

They were ready.

Following his lead, Clygon led them over the small hill. Then they saw it—the stronghold—where Toby had been held, where his *RiverHome* friends had been captives, where something terrible had happened to Mathilda. It rose up in front of them. But their eyes were set on the field down below—the trolls' meeting grounds where Toby had first seen Clygon in all of his power. Where Mathilda had been thrown onto the ground, broken and near death. Where Toby had planted the Sword, causing a huge explosion.

It was quiet. Too quiet. Given that a battle cry had gone out not more than an hour ago.

Mathilda pulled out her bow and arrow. Phoenix, Judah, and Deckor grabbed their swords. Clygon pulled out a sword as well. The Healer and Toby were completely dependent on their protection and Saaba's.

Clygon put a finger to his lips, signaling the need for quiet. They slowly made their way to the field in front of the stands to the spot where Toby had planted the Sword. He didn't need Clygon to guide him there. He sensed it. He felt it. And the big scar on the ground helped.

Phoenix, Deckor, Judah, and Mathilda formed a small circle facing outward as Clygon and Toby knelt down and began to dig. The Healer stood above them with a river elf light orb, trying to conceal it so as not to draw attention but in a way that provided light on the ground.

It hit Toby then how futile this whole Quest was. What were the chances of finding this really small piece of the Sword, in the dark, in the middle of enemy territory? It was madness.

The digging was intentionally slow as they needed to find the proverbial needle in a haystack. *What is the point of that proverb, anyway?* Only this time, it was like finding a pinhead in a pile of manure, as the mud gave off a rancid smell, not unlike the trolls did. Toby fought back a gag or two—as in a choke rather than a joke—as he continued to dig. The smell didn't seem to bother Clygon.

After several minutes, Clygon sat up on his knees.

"I'm afraid it's not here."

It was then that Toby felt something. Actually a few somethings. The compass in his pocket started to buzz. The Sword pieces in his backpack began to vibrate with energy. And... a tiny little piece of metal in the mud. The only reason he felt it, he was sure, was because it was a part of the Sword. Which meant it was a part of him.

He grabbed it with his thumb and finger and, without letting anyone else see, he quickly looked down and saw a tiny glow.

You found it, Toby! You found the good. I knew you would. You know what to do.

Sopha!

Instantly, and internally, Toby found himself in a battle. Everything in him wanted to keep the GOOD a secret so that he could repair the Sword and use the power for himself. To use it the way he saw fit.

Yes, Toby. Good thinking. Get it? Good thinking?

Sopha again.

The other part of him knew he needed, for the sake of his friends, to show them the piece and get out of there as quickly as possible and back to the giants.

Seriously Toby? All that power! It's waiting for you!

Sopha's tempting voice bored into his soul.

He sensed Mathilda turn to him.

"No!" she cried out.

But it was too late.

Toby stood up and power burst out of him, just like it had the last time when he had thrust the Sword in the ground on this very spot. But this time, rather than using that power against the trolls, it threw his friends about three feet away.

Immediately Judah, Phoenix, and Deckor were on their feet, running back to Toby. But Toby turned his hand toward them. The small Sword fragment created a force field, and they bounced off of it.

At that same moment, Clygon tried to jump Toby from behind, but the force field repelled him, as well.

Toby could hear Sopha laughing. A vile, grotesque laugh.

The fingers holding the Sword fragment started to burn. His arm felt like it was about to break off.

Toby.

The voice came gently.

Let it go, Toby. For GOOD-ness sake, let it go.

No! Don't do it, Toby. Grab! Optimize! Obl—

The smell of Christmas broke through the noise and the pain and the screaming of his friends.

Let it go. His grandpa's voice was urgently calm.

"Let it go? But… what about the Sword? What about *RiverHome?* What about the giants?"

Yesss, Toby. Good questionssss… You must hang on to…

Toby felt like he was about to explode.

It's okay, Toby. Let it go. The GOOD will find you!

Toby looked at the small fragment, seemingly burning a hole in his fingers. He could see his friends trying to get to him, the power of the force field pushing them back like a giant gust of wind.

He let out a huge scream. Pain shot through his fingers, up his arm, and out at his friends. Thankfully, his scream warned them, giving them just enough time to duck as an orange-blue wave of power splashed over them.

He fell to his knees. He looked at his fingers. The fragment was gone. Burned up. The GOOD was lost. Hope was lost.

He curled in on himself. He'd failed. He let his friends down. He let himself down. He let the Christmas Giant down. They'd never repair the Sword now.

He wept bitterly.

The Healer ran to him and began working on his hand and arm. Mathilda, Deckor, Phoenix, Judah, and Clygon slowly climbed to their feet, assessed the damage caused them by the force field, gathered their weapons, and joined the Healer.

The whole field had gone deathly silent. The small group of friends, damaged and battered, stood in quiet shock.

A torchlight caught Clygon's attention. Then another one. And soon, the field was lit up with torches, revealing Plythar… and hundreds of trolls… and Oliver and Evy, chains attached to their legs and hands, being prodded onto the field by Lucas.

Plythar stepped forward.

"Welcome home, Clygon. We've been waiting for you."

19. Finding the G…

"How did you know we would be here?" Clygon asked.

Plythar nodded his head toward Lucas.

"Our new giant ally, Lucas here, filled us in. Once we knew you were looking for a fragment of the Sword, it was a no-brainer."

"I thought you weren't going to tell them about the missing piece!" Clygon yelled at Lucas.

Lucas shrugged. "Needs must."

Plythar, surprised by what he'd just heard, decided to let it go. He was smart enough to know he couldn't trust his enemies, even if they seemed to be on the same side. He had more pressing matters.

The trolls slowly formed a circle around the river elves and Clygon, forcing them closer and closer together.

"So the battle horns we heard earlier, they were for us?" Clygon asked.

Plythar's eyes blinked, confused. "Battle horns?"

"Were you expecting someone else?" Clygon asked.

The troll soldiers began to look around nervously.

Lucas took a step forward.

"Nice bluff, little troll. But it won't work. Now, if you would be kind enough to hand over the Sword and the GOOD fragment, we can lock you up, and I can get to bed. It's been a long, exhausting trip. And we need to head back home soon."

A troll soldier prodded Clygon in the back with a sword, moving him in the direction of Toby, still under the care of the Healer.

As Clygon leaned down to give Toby a hand up, an arrow lodged itself in the troll soldier's shoulder. *Say that fast ten times!* Another embedded itself in the knee of the troll standing next to Plythar, knocking him to the ground. A third arrow hit Lucas on his wrist. But it didn't seem to faze him. He pulled it out as if it were a sliver.

But now it was mass chaos. Wolves ran in, taking big bites out of troll flesh. Arrows rained down on the trolls as river elves, led by Donold, ran out of the darkness, yelling with swords drawn. Ogres, following behind their Commander, Oreea, came from the left. Oreea herself ran toward Judah, hugged and kissed him, and handed him a sword. Drones above dropped rocks onto the trolls.

Clovor and Johanna rushed to Phoenix, Mathilda, and Deckor, pulling them back into the darkness. Clygon crouched over Toby and the Healer, waiting for a moment to move to safety.

Judah ran to Oliver and Evy, assuming that two giants chained up by the trolls must be on the side of the river elves, quickly cut the chains off of them, and then headed back to join Oreea. Evy tackled Lucas, who was none too happy about it. Oliver ran over to Clygon, Toby, and the Healer. He picked up the Healer and said, "You two, stay here. I'll be back in a moment."

The trolls quickly recovered from the surprise attack and took control of the fight. There were far more of them than there were river elves, wolves, and ogres. And they kept coming.

Plythar headed up the hill a ways to the grandstands so that he could see the battlefield and yell out orders.

As Clygon continued to hover over Toby, he said, "Now would be a good time to find the GOOD."

"But I lost it! I lost it!"

No! You didn't! The Christmas Giant whispered to him.

"Toby!" It was Mathilda. She pulled herself out of Clovor's grip and ran to him.

"Listen to me. What if you're the key to the GOOD? What if the GOOD is in you?"

"Huh?"

An arrow landed dangerously close to them.

"Go!" Clygon yelled at her. "I think I know what you mean. We've got this."

"We do?" Toby asked.

Oliver was back, standing over them, swatting arrows away from them.

"What do you need me to do?"

"Protect us. We need to find the GOOD, and I think it's going to take a while!" Clygon said.

Oliver picked up a troll rushing at him and threw him fifty feet into a group of five other trolls. That would buy them some time.

"Do you remember Harold's poem?" Clygon shouted.

A troll ran past screaming, with Saaba on his heels. *Did Saaba just wink at them?*

"What does that poem have to do..." asked Toby, still dazed.

"Do. You. Remember. It!" Clygon was running out of patience.

"I do," offered Oliver.

Former enemies they may be...

A human and a troll.

The Sword in peril...

On a Quest they go.

To find the GOOD...

And save the world.

Toby and Clygon stared at him.

"We had to memorize it as kids." Oliver smiled at them.

"Still not a great poem," Toby muttered. "How does that help us?" An arrow whizzed by his ear, landing in the foot of a troll.

"We're to do this together, Toby. The GOOD is in us, and somehow we have to figure out what that means."

The compass in Toby's pocket sprang to life, buzzing so frantically it felt as if it would ignite into flames. Toby pulled it out, and he and Clygon found themselves drawn into it.

"What else can I do?" Oliver shouted, staring down a troll who wisely turned and ran the other way.

Above the fighting they could hear Plythar yelling. "Get that Baxter kid! Get Clygon! Get that Sword!"

"Just buy us time. We need cover," Clygon answered.

"I have just the thing." Oliver reached into his pocket and pulled out a purple Ostern egg. He quickly squeezed it, and a purple smoke started to seep out of it.

"This is a fog of confusion. When anyone comes near, it discombobulates them. That's a great word, isn't it? Anyway, I need to be out in front of the fog to make sure none of our friends get too close to it. It will buy you about thirty minutes."

As Oliver headed away, the deep purple fog enveloped them, acting almost like a curtain. A loud, rushing wind-type sound surrounded them, adding to the noise of the battle outside of the fog.

"Now what?" Toby yelled.

"We need to figure out the GOOD."

"Meaning?"

"We need to discover what each letter on this compass means. That will, in turn, guide us in repairing the Sword," Clygon explained-shouted.

"How do we do that?"

"I guess we… ah… start throwing out words that begin with G and see if the compass likes any of them."

"But that could take forever!" Toby complained.

"Obviously, we want to narrow it down to words that somehow define GOOD."

"So?"

"So let's just yell out G words and watch the compass! I don't know what else to do," Clygon shouted.

By now, they were fully encircled by the fog. A faint light glowed from it so that they could see. The compass, as well, provided light.

"Good!" yelled out Clygon.

"You can't use the word you're describing to describe the word!"

"Oh. Yah. Of course. How about… Goodness?"

"Again," Toby said, "you can't use the word you're describing."

"Goiter… Ghost… Gaggle… Gum… Gobsmacked… Ginger… Goofball…"

"What are you doing?" Toby asked. "What do any of those words have to do with GOOD?"

"Well, then, you give it a try!"

The compass continued its frantic buzzing.

Toby thought. And thought some more.

"Gape… Grape… Gunnysack…"

"Gunnysack? Really?"

"Wait… I think the fog of confusion is confusing us a bit." Toby took a deep breath.

"Think of someone good. What's a word, starting with G, that would describe that person?"

Clygon scratched his big nose.

"My adoptive parents, Prothar, Sythar, and Thytar, are good. They are kind…"

"That begins with a K…"

"Giving…"

The compass began to slow.

"Keep at it. You're on the right track."

"Exceptionally giving?"

"Oh… so close," Toby said. "It's barely ticking. Wait. I've got it! The river elf grandma. You know. I don't think I knew her name! Anyway, Mathilda and I were talking about what a good woman she was. She was… she was… so… Generous. She freely gave of her time and herself. She always went out of the way to make us feel cared for. I always felt better about myself around her."

"Me, too!" Clygon said.

The compass stopped. Pointing at the G.

"Generous. That's it!"

Clygon and Toby jumped up and down together.

The compass began to move again.

20. Finding the …OO…

Something rolled past Toby and stopped a few feet from him.

"Gross! Is that a troll's head?"

Clygon walked over and gently kicked it with his foot.

"Is that what it means to say that heads will roll?" Toby asked.

"Wow. That's really dark, Toby."

Clygon bent over and slowly reached out to touch whatever it was. Then he picked it up.

"Nope. Just a big rock. Probably dropped by the drones."

He tossed it through the fog.

"Hey! Watch it! You almost knocked my head off with that thing!"

"Sorry, Deckor! We can't see you through the fog."

"Well… hurry up in there."

Clygon walked back to Toby, and the two of them watched the wildly spinning compass. The battle sounds all around them.

"Okay. O words. How about… Okay?"

"To be GOOD is to be okay?" Toby asked. "Seems a bit lame."

"Okay. Then be my guest, Mr O man!" Clygon muttered.

"Sorry. You're right. If we want to find the GOOD, then perhaps we need to be more open to each other's ideas…"

The compass stopped on the first O.

"Wait. What did I just say?" Toby asked.

The compass slowly started spinning.

"You said that if we want to find the GOOD, then we need to be more… more…"

"Open!" Toby shouted.

The compass stopped.

"Open?" they both asked together.

"What does Open have to do with being GOOD?" Clygon asked.

"How about—being Open to others. As in, being honest with who you are. Genuine. Not pretending to be someone else."

"Yeah. Like not doctoring your photo on your TrollFace page," Clygon thought he said to himself.

Toby stared at Clygon. "Really? You have a TrollFace page?"

The compass stayed rooted on the first O.

"Got it! Generous. Open," Clygon said, trying to save his troll face.

The compass began to spin again.

"How about…" Clygon was thinking out loud. "How about… Opulence?"

"What does gas have to do with being GOOD?"

"Not flatulence," Clygon laughed. "Opulence. Having great wealth. Being successful, perhaps?"

The compass kept spinning.

"I guess you can be successful and wealthy and not necessarily GOOD?" Toby asked.

"Odorless," Clygon said.

"It does help," Toby said.

They stared at the compass.

"What is it about GOOD people that makes them attractive? The kind of people that you want to be around?" Toby asked.

"They're fun?"

The compass slowed.

"Okay. You're on to something. What makes them fun?"

"They're happy… positive…"

The compass slowed to the point where it seemed to will the word out of them.

"The Christmas Giant!" Toby said.

"What about him?"

"He always hopes for the best. He's… Ophthalmologist? Origami?"

"Optimistic? Is that the word you're looking for?" asked Clygon.

The compass stopped on the second O.

"Yes! Generous. Open. Optimistic. One more."

"One more what?"

It was Plythar.

21. Finding the… D

Toby and Clygon froze, hoping Plythar wouldn't see them. But not only did he see them, he walked right up to them.

"You boys wouldn't happen to know where my sword is, would you? There seems to be a battle waging around us and I can't for the life of me find my weapon." He looked around helplessly, holding his sword in his right hand.

"He's confused," Clygon whispered-shouted into Toby's ear. "Maybe we can use this to our advantage. But we have to act quickly before the confusion wears off."

"What are you thinking?"

"Mr Plythar, sir," Clygon said to Plythar, who was on his knees looking for his sword, still in his right hand. He looked up at Clygon.

"I think we can help you find your sword."

"Oh, that would be so very kind of you, young man. And what is your name?"

"Clygon."

Plythar's eyes widened. A scowl ran across his face.

Wow… that scowl literally ran across his face, Toby thought.

"Do I know you?" he asked.

Clygon ignored him.

"Mr Plythar, sir. Your sword is on the other side of that purple curtain. Once you get out there, call out for your friend, Oliver the Giant, and tell him that you want to surrender."

"Why would I want to do that?"

"To stop the fighting," Toby said. "To stop trolls from getting hurt."

Plythar shook his head, seemingly to knock the fog out of it.

"We need to get him back into that fog and out to Oliver!" Toby said, grabbing Plythar and leading him toward the edges of the fog.

Plythar began to resist. He raised his sword.

But then a big hand reached in and pulled Plythar through the fog back onto the battlefield.

They could hear Plythar's voice.

"Are you Mr Oliver? Some nice... young men... said that I should... ah..."

A large roar went up. Toby and Clygon could hear rather than see a group of trolls rushing to the aid of Plythar. They could hear sword against sword followed by a shout of victory.

"It didn't work!" Plythar shouted through the fog, his voice fading. Apparently he was being led back to a safer place.

The battle continued around them.

Clygon noticed the fog beginning to thin.

"That was risky!" Toby said.

"It almost wor… What?"

"Look at the compass. It slowed when I said, risky. What are words for risky?"

"Chancy… Precarious…"

"It needs to start with D!"

They both looked at each other. The pressure of finding the D before the fog ran out was getting to them. They couldn't think.

"Wait," Toby said, "I remember watching a show on Amazon about two boys whose dad had died."

"That sounds depressing," Clygon said. "Hey, that's a D word."

"The boys' dad kept appearing to them to teach them life lessons…"

"So he wasn't really dead? Hey, that's a D word, too."

"It was metaphorical. Anyway, would you just listen. He would often say to his boys, 'Be Dangerously Good.'"

The compass slowed to a crawl.

"But that seems to be an oxymoron. Can Dangerous and GOOD go together?"

"I think he meant that they should take risks in doing good—that they should be bold in practicing goodness... Daring..."

The compass stopped.

"Daring! It's Daring!" Toby shouted. "G—Generous. O—Open. O—Optimistic. D—Daring. GOOD. We found the GOOD!"

"Now what?" Clygon asked.

"Whatever it is," Oliver shouted through the quickly thinning fog, "you have minutes to figure it out. The fog has almost dissipated..."

"Did he say constipated?" Toby asked.

"Dissipated—the fog has almost disappeared," Clygon said patiently. "Let's fix the Sword!"

Toby poured out the Sword fragments onto the ground. He and Clygon quickly tried to piece them together. It was like a jigsaw puzzle. Toby hated jigsaw puzzles.

It took a few minutes, but now the Sword lay in front of them, waiting for whatever was supposed to happen to happen to heal it and reconnect all the pieces.

"What do we do now?" Clygon stepped back, looking at the Sword. The fog was almost gone, and they could see that they were encircled by river elves, wolves, ogres, Oliver and Evy, and some of the trolls from the Resistance. Surrounding their friends were hundreds of trolls, so far kept at bay by river elf arrows and rock bombs from the drones above.

Toby put his ear down to the Sword, as if listening to it. Clygon noticed Toby's hands beginning to glow. He looked at his own hands and saw that they, too, were glowing a bright blue.

"What's going…"

"Shhh…" Toby said.

He continued to listen to the Sword and then repeated what he was hearing:

Passion… heart… metal… unite!

Forge a Sword!

Protect with Light!

"What?" Clygon asked.

Passion… heart… metal… unite!

Forge a Sword!

Protect with Light!

"That's that lame poem you made up back in Harold's home…"

"Take my hand!" Toby shouted. The fog was gone, but the roar of the wind had increased.

He grabbed Clygon's hand.

He placed their hands on the hilt of the Sword. Light flowed through their hands down into the empty spaces between the fragments, pulling them together.

"That vial Rainie gave us. Pour it on the Sword!"

Clygon desperately rummaged in his tunic. It proved a difficult task with just one hand but he finally retrieved the vial. He poured the liquid onto the Sword.

"Oops!" he shouted. "I was supposed to touch the hilt and the point of the Sword with it, not pour it out."

But the liquid flowed like a small river into the crevices between the Sword fragments.

The intensity of the light increased. The hurricane winds around them grew deafening. The battle around them slowed and then halted as if everyone was frozen in time.

"What's going on?" Clygon shouted.

"We're combining our hearts and passion to heal the Sword… but I'm missing something. The tip isn't coming together."

"That's because it's missing the GOOD!" Clygon yelled. "Passion and heart aren't enough. We need the GOOD."

Toby's right pointer finger and thumb began to burn. He looked at them and just barely saw it. Imprinted on them was the OOD. The Sword piece had burned itself into his finger and thumb.

Suddenly behind them, they heard Plythar screaming:

"STOP THEM! NOW! BEFORE THEY FIX THAT SWORD!"

The trolls seemed to wake up from their trance and rushed the river elves, the ogres, and the wolves.

"We can't hold them, Toby!" Clovor yelled. "There are too many of them. What are you waiting for?"

Clygon placed his other hand on the Sword.

Toby placed his finger and thumb on the tiny spot missing the OOD, right next to the G on the Sword.

"Generous…Open… Optimistic... Daring…" Toby and Clygon said together.

"Generous… Open… Optimistic… Daring…"

"NOOOOOO!" Plythar shouted.

Light exploded out of the Sword, rolling under the river elf army and their allies and bursting out of the ground, throwing trolls hundreds of feet into the air.

Another wave of trolls rushed them.

"Hold your positions!" Donold yelled to his troops.

Another explosion of light and energy from the Sword threw more trolls into the air.

Toby and Clygon slowly lifted the Sword, holding it above their heads. Lightning flashed out of it like Zeus's lightning bolt.

"For the GOOD!" Toby shouted. "Surrender now, and you will be treated with goodness and decency."

Trolls dropped their swords and fell to their knees.

Plythar ran down into his army, kicking them and screaming at them to fight.

The river elf army cautiously held their weapons in battle-ready position.

With the exception of the hurricane-like wind emanating from the Sword, silence fell on the battlefield. An eerie silence.

After several moments, Donold turned to Clovor and said, "Something's wrong. I don't like this."

At that moment, Plythar raised his fingers to his mouth and let out a loud, long whistle.

"Oh no!" Clygon said.

22. You Good?

"Oh no? What do you mean, oh no?" Toby asked frantically.

Before Clygon could answer, the ground began to shake underneath them. Loud booming from behind the trolls grew louder and louder. From up behind the trolls... *A mountain? A one-eyed mountain?...* rose up. An enormous head. With one big eye in the middle of it, glowing a sickening red. Attached to a more enormouser body. *Yes... I know that's not a word, Author! Not now!* With huge, massive arms and hands, both of which looked like Thor's hammerhead.

The trolls stood to their feet and began to cheer.

The river elves and their allies fell back. Quickly.

The Sword had lost its glow, probably because Toby and Clygon were distracted by the mammoth creature in front of them.

"What? Who?" Toby could hardly get the words out.

"That," Clygon said, "is Teddy."

"Teddy? As in Teddy bear? Seriously?"

"Well, actually, he used to be..."

"Spit it out, Clygon! We don't have all day."

"I found him as a baby, abandoned by his tribe. Not sure why they left him. But what I did know was that he could be trained to be our secret weapon should our enemies ever gain the upper hand. He was just a boy when you were here last, Toby. Apparently, Plythar decided to do what I had planned on doing. He has been training Teddy for battle."

"Is he a…"

"Cyclops? Yes. We thought that, like the giants, they had disappeared."

"Apparently not," deadpanned Toby.

By now, Teddy was standing across the field with the trolls, facing Toby, Clygon, the river elf soldiers, and their allies.

Donold and Clovor eased their way over to Toby and Clygon.

"What do we need to know?" Donold asked.

Toby's head started spinning. Actually, his head wasn't moving but it felt like his head was spinning. *What good would GOOD do them now?* He was exhausted. His entire body screamed at him to lay down… *or is it lie…never mind…* and sleep.

He heard Clygon say, "… actually a gentle…"

Only to have his words drowned out by a loud roar from Teddy, who beat his chest and stomped his feet, causing a slight earthquake underneath them. He could feel Teddy's energy building, waiting to pounce on them and crush them.

"Did you think," came Plythar's voice across the field, "that I am as thick as Clygon? No offense…"

"Some taken," Clygon muttered.

"Did you think that drawing a line in the sand or singing Christmas carols would in any way defeat me or the trolls? And really, all of that drama, Toby. Lightening sparks from the Sword. Glowing hands. Power exploding out of you. You're a one-trick pony. And all this work to find the good. What a waste. As you will learn in a moment, good is never good enough. Good is the weak sibling of GREAT, and now you will see GREAT!"

"Oh yeah!" Toby yelled, holding the faintly glowing Sword up in the air. "Great without GOOD is only… um… is just…"

The trolls laughed.

Toby began to glow. Hot, angry red. With a tinge of humiliated orange. But this time, the Sword didn't respond.

"Toby!" Clovor yelled at him. "You good?"

He put down the Sword.

"Not really. What good is GOOD if that cyclops is going to mash us into potato land?"

"Huh?" Clygon asked.

"Sorry. What's the plan? How do we harness the GOOD to get us out of this mess?"

Teddy took a massive step toward them. Then stopped. His massive red eye focused in on Clygon. And if it's possible, the eye looked confused.

"Listen to me carefully," Clygon said. "None of the trolls know this, but I befriended Teddy. He was the only friend I ever had. I determined not to turn him into a fighting machine. I protected him from the other trolls, always telling them that he wasn't ready to train for battle. He seems to recognize me even though it's been years, and I look a lot different. The trolls have obviously turned him into a monster. But that's not his nature. If I can somehow get up onto his back and speak to him…"

"What good will that do?"

"Every time we said goodnight, I always said to him, 'You are a good friend.' If he hears my voice saying that, maybe I can bring him back to himself."

He huddled with Toby, Donold, and Clovor and offered an idea.

"That's it? That's the plan?" Toby asked. "It will never work."

"Just like a line in the sand wouldn't work? Or singing Christmas carols wouldn't work?" Donold asked. "I've seen enough from you, Toby Baxter, to know that you are GOOD. And by that, I mean your spirit is right, and you're ready for this."

"It's a GOOD plan, Toby," Clygon said. "It's got all of the GOOD in it. It's motivated by Generosity—fighting for the good of everyone. It's an Open, honest plan as it seeks to bring out the real Teddy. It's certainly Optimistic—rooted in hope. And, let's face it, Toby, it's Daringly GOOD!"

With that, Donold and Clovor made a big show of calling the river elf soldiers, their allies, along with Oliver and Evy, into retreat, leaving Toby and Clygon isolated.

"So… leave it to the river elves to leave it to the kids to fight their battles. Typical!" Plythar spit the words out. *Or is it spat out the… never mind.*

Teddy took another massive step and then stopped.

"You can either surrender right now, hand over the Sword, and live, not comfortably, of course, but live," Plythar shouted. "Or our cyclops friend here can pile-drive you into the ground. Which will it be?"

Toby lifted the Sword. It began to glow. As did he.

"Go!" Plythar shouted at Teddy.

It would only take the cyclops about four big steps before he would squish Toby and Clygon into the ground.

One step… two steps… three…

"Now!" Clygon shouted.

Toby rushed Teddy with the Sword aimed at a kneecap, lightning sparks blasting out of it. Teddy brushed him away like a mosquito.

Distracted by Toby, the cyclops didn't see Clygon running off to his side, out of the line of his limited vision. Because all of the trolls were off to the other side of Teddy's massive frame, they couldn't see what was happening in front of them.

"For the GOOD!" Toby shouted as he jumped up and planted the Sword into the ground right in front of Teddy. An explosion rippled through the ground, slightly knocking Teddy off balance for a moment.

"For the GOOD!" yelled Clygon as he jumped up onto the back of the cyclops and began climbing toward his neck.

Then… a cry from Mathilda:

"Toby, watch out!"

But it was too late. Teddy swatted Toby into the air. He landed with a thud on the ground twenty feet away, limp and lifeless.

23. Page Break

"Toby. Come on! You need to see this!"

Toby was standing on a cement bridge over a stream flowing toward the edge of a cliff a few feet in front of him. Off to his left, he saw a huge pavilion used for picnics. On the other side of that pavilion, about a block or so away, was a Dairy Queen. He knew down a ways from the pavilion was a bandstand and a huge park area. At the end of the bridge, Sid was yelling and gesturing at him.

"Toby. Stop daydreaming. Let's go. You really need to see this!"

Toby followed Sid down a sidewalk with a road to their left, the pavilion to the left of the road, and a waist-high wall to their right. On the other side of that wall, down below, the waterfall splashed into a stream that ran through a hilly, forested area down to the Mississippi River.

Sid led him to a stairway that would take them to the bottom of the falls. There, at the foot of the waterfall, a small bridge crossed the stream to a pathway leading down to the river.

"I told you the waterfall near *RiverHome* looked familiar…"

Minnehaha Falls? What am I doing here?

Toby reached out and grabbed Sid by the arm.

"What are we doing here?"

Sid stopped. He looked Toby in the eyes.

"Are you okay, Toby? We're here on the last-week-of-school-trip with our 7th-grade class."

"Last week of school? But... but... we're on spring break in Hawaii..."

"Wow. They said that you might have residual effects from your fall on that bike ride, but seriously, talk about delayed reaction."

"Did I crash?"

"You're starting to scare me, Toby. Come back to earth. Come on. Let's go down to the stream. Maybe we can find the opening to *RiverHome!*"

Sid was already racing down the stairs when Toby noticed a tall, black-skinned, bald-headed man, serving ice-cream at a small ice-cream cart. He was wearing a shirt with white and pastel pink stripes, a white apron, and white pants. He had a pencil tucked behind his left ear, reading glasses hanging around his neck, and a notebook tucked in the pocket of his apron.

Toby crossed the street and got in line. When it was his turn, Author said, "What can I... Toby? What are you doing here?"

Author was obviously discombobulated.

"That's what I'd like to know. And if you don't know, that's kind of a problem, isn't it?"

Author quickly hung an **Out to Lunch, Back in 30 Minutes** sign on the cart, to the groans of the five kids behind Toby. "No worries, kids. Free ice cream when I get back!"

"Walk with me," Author said to Toby.

They headed toward the steps Sid had run down a few moments earlier and climbed down to the bottom of the waterfall.

As the spray misted their faces, Toby saw, off to his left, Sid standing on the other side of the small bridge that crossed over the stream. To his right was a wall.

Sid was right. How had he missed this?

"Is this the setting for *RiverHome?*" Toby asked Author.

But Author was busy paging through his notebook.

A group of students about his age tried to move around him to cross the bridge.

"Toby? Toby Baxter?"

And there she was.

Rainie.

The mist from the waterfall made her look like an angel. He hadn't seen her in a year. She'd grown up in that time, just as he had done. But she was still the girl he had a crush on. Her blonde hair fell onto her shoulders. Her cat-green eyes almost hypnotized him. The small mole, just above her top lip, a bit off to the right, added to the cuteness. *Added to the cuteness? Get a grip, Toby!*

"I… uh… Rainie? I…um…"

"You didn't think I knew you, did you."

"No. I… we… well… we never actually talked."

She took a pen out of her small backpack.

"Here's my phone number. Call me!"

She wrote it down on his hand. Her hands felt so soft. So warm. So… *Get. A. Grip.*

He watched as she and her friends crossed the bridge. Sid was furiously pointing at her, making sure Toby had seen her. Though Sid had never met her, he'd recognize her anywhere from the way Toby dreamily talked about her. All. The. Time.

"I think I've figured out the problem, Toby," Author said, interrupting the moment. "My bad. I had a few thoughts on a new story idea and jotted them down without putting a hard space between your current story and my notes. So… the current story ran into the new sto—"

"New story? Current story? What are you talking about?"

"You know how, on a computer, you put a page break when you want to start a new page or a new chapter or a new story? Well…"

But Toby was no longer paying attention to him. His eyes were on Rainie. As he watched her and her friends walk downstream, he saw something move on the hill next to them. Instantly, he knew what he was seeing, but it was too late. A troll arm grabbed Rainie, and as Sid ran to help her, another troll arm grabbed him and the troll arms and Rainie and Sid disappeared into a portal.

Toby started to run across the bridge.

"Rainie! Sid!"

"… if I just draw a hard line under the current story, that should get you back into…"

Toby stopped. He turned to Author.

"Author! Wait!"

"Line drawn. I'll also write 'Page break' just to be safe," Author said as he wrote **Page break** in his journal.

24. For the GOOD

Toby slowly opened his eyes. His head ached. He felt the side of his head. A small knot... *why is it called a knot when it's a bump?... from something... what was it?*

Mathilda was on her knees trying to hold him up by his left shoulder, thankfully, as his right shoulder was screaming at him. Clovor was holding the Sword in his left hand with both of her hands. Judah, Deckor, Phoenix, and Donold stood over him with swords drawn. Behind them stood the Healer, Oliver, and Evy. He could hear Oreea shouting orders from somewhere off to the side.

As his mind cleared he saw Clygon trying to scale a moving mountain. It had a name. *Freddy? Betty? Lenny?*

"Teddy!" Clovor shouted.

How does she do that?

But she wasn't saying it to Toby. She was shouting it at the moving mountain. As it turned toward them Toby saw the huge red eye in the middle of its even huger head. It all came back to him. He'd taken a massive hit from that massive hand attached to that massive cyclops body.

The trolls were chanting Teddy's name. Plythar and Lucas stood with them, waiting for the moment when Teddy would end this battle and they could all get on with their lives.

Clygon took advantage of the temporary distraction Clovor had provided and raced as quickly as he could up Teddy's back.

Teddy once again moved toward Toby and his friends. Toby could feel his energy returning, made visible from the increasingly glowing Sword. Plythar noticed and shouted at the cyclops to get a move on.

But suddenly Teddy stopped. Dead in his tracks, metaphorically speaking. His shoulders slumped a bit as he reached his massive arm up to his neck and gently grabbed Clygon, then held Clygon up close to his red eye with both hands. Teddy's shoulders began to jump up and down followed by a huge, mountainous laugh. He hugged Clygon, held him up in front of his red eye again, and then hugged him once more.

"Teddy is a good friend to Clygon. Teddy is a good friend to Clygon," Teddy yelled joyfully.

Lucas turned to Plythar with a look of panic and outrage. Plythar simply looked confused.

Teddy gently placed Clygon on the ground and turned his ginormous red eye onto Plythar and Lucas.

"Teddy is a good friend to Clygon. You will be good friends to Clygon, too!"

He took one step toward the trolls, all of whom dropped their swords and ran in panic.

"It's not good to fight. It's not good to hate," Teddy yelled after them. "Come back. Let's be friends!"

Plythar didn't stick around, either. He moved remarkably fast for a troll.

The river elves and the ogres let out a loud cheer and ran to encircle Teddy, chanting his name. Clygon grabbed him by the hand and moved him through the crowd, making sure the cyclops didn't step on anyone, and led him over to Toby.

By now, the Sword was back to normal. Toby, with the help of Mathilda, stood up and, as Teddy approached him, bowed to him, almost falling over, still dizzy from the bump on his head.

"No need to bow, friend of Clygon. Any friend of Clygon is a friend of Teddy's. If he says you are good, you are good! And Teddy is sorry for knocking your brains out. It was a mistake."

"Teddy talks like you do," Oliver whispered to Evy.

Teddy reached out his hand to pat Toby on the head, but Clygon stopped him. "Toby doesn't need another headache, Teddy."

"Not so fast," Oliver cried out.

He and Evy grabbed Lucas, who was trying to slink off without being noticed, which isn't easy for a giant.

"You have a lot to answer for, Lucas. You've brought great harm on the land and great shame onto the giants. Tonight, we will rest and celebrate with our new friends. Tomorrow, we will head back home."

Oliver turned to Toby and Clygon.

"Toby. Clygon. As healers of the Sword, will you accompany us back to the *Tikvah Mountains?* I know Harold, Pumpernickel, and all of the giants will want to honor what you have done today."

"Of course," Clygon answered for both of them. But something was gnawing at Toby. *Gnawing! That's a good word for it.* Something about Rainie. His Rainie. Not the giant's Rainie. And Sid.

That night, Toby, Clygon, the river elves, the ogres, the drones, the wolves, Teddy, Oliver and Evy, sat around a fire and enjoyed a feast of food they managed to plunder from the now-abandoned troll stronghold.

Clygon told them of their adventures leading up to their dramatic showdown with Plythar.

Toby, although still woozy from the blow to the head, told them about his bike ride into the cloud in Hawaii and ending up in the mountain.

Oliver and Evy filled them in on the challenges the giants were facing back home, obviously concerned about what was happening after Lucas led his revolt.

Lucas sat silently through all of it.

Mathilda focused her attention on Toby. "Before you tell us, again, that you didn't do anything, that Clygon did all of the work by climbing up Teddy's back…"

Toby's face turned red.

"You did exactly what you needed to do. You found the GOOD. You, along with Clygon, healed the Sword. That was your

Quest, Toby. By doing so, you saved the land. And more importantly, you discovered what it means for you to be GOOD."

Toby wanted to argue but his head was screaming at him.

Teddy jumped in—which would have been quite dangerous if he had done it literally—and told them about living with the trolls and how much he despised fighting. He expressed to them how much he loved Clygon and, now, all of his new friends. Toby noticed that the red had eased in Teddy's eye, showing his eye to be a dark gray.

But then a cloud passed over Teddy's face. Metaphorically, but he was tall enough for a low-hanging cloud to do so literally if a cloud had meandered by.

"What is it, friend?" Clygon asked.

But before Teddy could answer, Evy said, "Evy wants Teddy to know that the giants welcome him as an honorary giant. We want you to come live and work with us."

Teddy looked at Oliver, who nodded an enthusiastic yes. He looked at Lucas, who shrugged.

The cloud over Teddy's face was replaced by sunshine, even though it was now late at night.

"Teddy said, 'Yes!'"

25. A Giant Send-Off

He woke with a full body ache. Everything hurt. Especially his right shoulder. His headache had lessened a bit. Silver linings. *Silver linings?* He'd bumped his head one too many times on this trip.

Apparently, he had fallen asleep during the festivities last night. The last thing he remembered was something about Teddy living with the giants.

"Not to worry," Clygon said, popping his head into the room where Toby had been sleeping. And apparently, Saaba as well, who was curled up next to him. "The party broke up right after you fell asleep. We have a long journey ahead of us, and we all needed to get some rest. Breakfast is ready, by the way, and then we need to leave."

Toby easily found the latrine—*you simply can't hide that troll stink!*—and then headed into a large outdoor eating area. River elves and ogres sat around square tables, eating more of the food left by the trolls when they retreated.

At the center table sat Clovor, Phoenix, Deckor, Judah, Oreea, Mathilda, Donold, Johanna, and the Healer. They motioned for Toby to join them.

Suddenly, they heard a noise coming from the bushes behind them. Blythar and ten of his trolls burst through, ready to fight. Phoenix jumped up, put his hands in the air, and said, "Just in time for breakfast."

"Shoot. Did we miss the fight? What happened?" Blythar said, genuinely disappointed that they'd arrived too late.

Clygon gave them the Cliff Notes version as everyone dug into their breakfast.

"We won't be going with you to the *Tikvah Mountains*, Toby," Clovor said, as they finished eating. Before he could protest, she put up her hand. "We need to get back and make sure *RiverHome* and *Ogreton Heights* are safe. We don't know what Plythar might be up to next."

"And," Phoenix interrupted, unable to control himself, "to make plans for a gigantic three-day festival with our new giant friends. Get it. Gigantic. Giants. I can't wait to see the looks on the faces of our river elf friends when they see giants for the first time."

"What is it, Toby?" Judah asked, seeing Toby's expression.

"I… uh… I'm sorry to hear about Grandma."

"That's very kind of you, Toby," Mathilda said. "We miss her so much. But we're happy to know she is with our river elf ancestors."

"She helped us find the GOOD," Clygon said, walking up behind Toby.

After breakfast, the river elves, ogres, wolves, Resistance trolls, and drones said their goodbyes to Toby, Clygon, Oliver, Evy, and Teddy.

"We're sorry we didn't get much time with you, Toby. Your Quest took you on a slightly different path," Clovor said.

Toby, feeling himself grimacing from the ongoing pain in his shoulder, said, "I'm not sure why, but I don't think the Quest is over yet. Plus, there are still four words on the Sword. That must mean something, right?"

They shared hugs, handshakes, and pats on the back and headed their separate ways. But not before Saaba got in one last sloppy kiss from the bottom of Toby's chin to the top of his head.

By the time they reached the *Tikvah Mountains,* word had spread that Lucas's plan had failed, evidenced by the fact that hundreds and hundreds of giants, led by Harold, met them outside! They all had cool sunglasses on to protect their eyes and something white-ish on their skin. *Sunscreen?*

Pumpernickel was the first to run to them. He put his massive arms around Toby and Clygon, giving them a giant hug.

"Another homonym," Clygon whispered.

To cheers and "Hail Toby Baxter! Hail Clygon! Hail Oliver! Hail Evy!" Harold led them back into the heart of the mountain to a huge feast waiting for them in the giant hall.

"Another hom—"

"I know," said Toby.

"It never gets old," Clygon said.

Before they entered the hall, Toby pulled Pumpernickel aside.

"What will happen to Lucas and to the others who rebelled against Harold?"

"We believe in restorative justice here, Toby."

"What does that mean?"

"It means that while there are always consequences to our actions, our goal and aim is to use our justice process to restore Lucas and the others to our giant family. It may take time. But I'm confident we can help them write a new story."

The feast, of course, was ginormous. But Toby had little appetite. The pain in his body made him feel nauseous.

After the festivities, Harold called for silence.

"My fellow giants, today we have much to be thankful for. We give thanks for the bounty of food we have just enjoyed."

Giant cheers.

"Don't say it," Toby whispered to Clygon.

"I had no intention of whispering 'homonym.'"

"We give thanks for our new friend, Teddy, who showed himself to be a good friend of the giants."

More cheering, causing Toby's lessened headache to unlessen, *if that's even a word!*

"We give thanks for the renewed alliance with our friends, the river elves and their allies, which we will celebrate with them at *RiverHome,* outside, in three weeks' time. At which time, we will embed the newly healed Sword once again in its proper home."

Lots of cheering.

"Toby Baxter! Clygon! Come up here, please."

To the loudest, giantest... *I know it's not a real word, but when in giant land...* cheer yet, Toby and Clygon made their way to the platform and stood next to Harold.

Pumpernickel joined them, handing the Sword to Toby.

The crowd fell silent.

Toby had never felt so uncomfortable before.

He held the Sword up, and as he did so, the giants began to hum. The humming was low. Almost a murmur. But it had a moving melody to it. The Sword began to glow. Toby could feel its energy filling his soul. His body. His mind. His heart.

"Toby, together with Clygon, you found the GOOD. By doing so, you healed the Sword. Which, in turn, will bring GOOD and healing back to the land. You have also reminded us that we are called to be GOOD to our neighbors. We have turned our backs on them long enough. It will be GOOD to reengage with the world."

The humming grew louder. Toby felt like he was about to pass out from the pain in his shoulder and his growing headache.

"Toby Baxter! Look at me!"

Toby turned to Harold.

"You have done much good, Toby. Most importantly, you proved yourself to be GOOD. As you go..."

Go? I'm going?

For some reason, Clygon took hold of the Sword with him.

"Be a HERO. Be WISE. Be GOOD."

Toby, barely able to keep his eyes open as the light from the Sword exacerbated his headache, as did big words like exacerbated, looked out at the crowd of giants.

Suddenly, they stretched out their hands toward him and began to sing a song in a language he didn't understand. But he knew they were blessing him. They were saying goodbye.

I'm proud of you, Toby. GOOD on you!

Lord Trut-Vater, aka the Christmas Giant, aka the voice of his Grandpa Baxter.

"Until we meet again, friend Toby," Clygon said as he took the Sword from him.

He heard a woman crying. *Evy?*

"Sid! Thomas! He's opening his eyes."

26. A Lo Ha

His mom stood over him with a hint of tears in her eyes. He was on a road, a bike next to him. His shoulder was killing him.

"Are you okay, son?" Thomas's face came into view, concern written all over it—but not literally.

"What happened? What am I doing on the ground?"

"We think you hit your brakes as we were going through that small patch of fog a moment ago…" Thomas began.

"Small patch of fog? A moment ago?"

"… from the way you're holding your shoulder, it appears that it took the brunt of the impact. But from the looks of that scratch on your helmet, you probably dinged your head as well."

Toby sat up. He stretched out his arm and moved his shoulder. It was sore, very sore and stiff, but not broken, thankfully. It already had a nice big bruise on it. *A battle scar! Cool. Wait! The stain?* He removed his helmet and checked his head. Outside of a dull headache, he felt okay, although he thought he felt a slight knot… *why do they call it a knot again?*

"To be on the safe side…" a new voice spoke; the tour guide. "… our van is on the way up to drive you to a hospital to check for a concussion."

"I don't think I need…"

"Sorry, Toby," Thomas said. "He's right. We want to make sure you're good for the rest of the trip."

Good? If they only knew!

While they waited for the van, Sid meandered over and sat next to Toby. "You seemed a bit surprised that your crash happened only a moment ago. Perhaps you were somewhere else today?" He flashed Toby his trademark big, goofy Sid smile.

"I'll tell you later," Toby said as the van pulled up.

As the van made its way down the mountain, Mom asked Toby if he remembered hitting his brakes. He nodded no. He wasn't sure she wanted to hear what he did remember. She wasn't all that keen on his trips to *RiverHome*. "Don't ever do anything like that again," she said, putting her arm around his very sore shoulder and squeezing it much too hard. "Oh. Sorry, honey," she said, feeling him tense up.

They spent a few hours at the hospital, but the scan confirmed that he was not concussed. He was released from the hospital and cleared to enjoy his vacation in Maui.

That night, Mom and Dad popped into Toby's hotel room to make sure he was all right. They brought two large pizzas with them. Toby's appetite assured them that he was fine.

But Mom watched him anxiously.

"Were you back in—what is the name of it—*RiverBed* again, Toby?" she asked with a fair amount of mom concern.

Toby stopped in midbite and said, "Ah... well... it's not *RiverBed*. It's *RiverHome* and... um... I..."

"How about," Dad jumped in, "we enjoy our time in Maui, and we chat about Toby's adventures when we get back home."

Mom was about to argue when Sid chimed in.

"Does anybody know if they allow a loud laugh in Hawaii or just aloha?"

When no one responded, Sid shrugged his shoulders and said, "Tough crowd."

After Mom and Dad left, Sid asked, "Were you? Were you back in *RiverHome?*"

Toby told the story but didn't finish as Sid had fallen asleep.

The next day, as Toby was snorkeling, that foul mood hit him again. As he watched the multi-colored fish swimming below him, he thought through the adventure he had just been on and the Quest for the GOOD. As a massive turtle swam by him, an insight hit him—metaphorically. While his foul mood may have been generated in part by changing hormones and increasing shots of testosterone, he realized that for months, he hadn't felt good about himself. He felt a bit ugly on the inside, and the growing number of pimples on his face didn't help. He didn't feel like he was good at many things, with the exception of the trumpet, which made him geeky rather than cool. Derrick and his minions still harassed him from time to time, and he felt powerless to stop them. And for the life of him he couldn't talk to a girl with the exception of a few monosyllabic noises—*whatever monosyllabic means.* The huge ocean added to his sense of insignificance.

And yet, Toby…

He could actually smell Christmas through his snorkel gear!

And yet, Toby, I see the GOOD in you. I believe in you.

That moment in the water started the turnaround. The foul mood gradually began to lift as their week in Hawaii moved on.

They spent an afternoon ziplining, with each zipline increasingly longer until the final one took them over a long valley. Toby screamed almost the whole way down, not out of fear, but out of sheer joy.

They visited the Maui Ocean Center enjoying the sea life and the amazing, immersive movie on whales.

Most of the week, however, was spent on the beach or in the ocean. Mom and Dad checked in only at meal times, giving Toby and Sid the freedom to explore and enjoy the beach as they wanted, as long as they kept an eye on each other while in the water.

On the way to the airport, they stopped at the *ABC Store* at *Whaler's Village* so that Toby could pick up several boxes of dark chocolate-covered macadamia nuts for Mrs Grayson, his youth pastor, his counselor, Grandma Baxter, and of course, for himself. Three boxes for himself.

Now, in his bed, back from Hawaii yesterday, Toby picked up *Of Mice and Men*. He hadn't read a page of it on the trip, so he had some reading to do over the weekend. It turns out it was not a horror story about an invasion of mice, but a story about two migrant workers. The book was only 112 pages, thankfully, so he should be able to get through the first three chapters by Sunday night.

He started reading but found it hard to keep his eyes open, even though it was 5 pm Hawaii time, 9 pm Minneapolis time. *Must be the jetlag.*

He got through Chapter 1, sighed, closed the book, and put it on his nightstand. He turned off the light. He closed his eyes.

And then he started to giggle.

Do they allow a loud laugh in Hawaii or just a-lo-ha?

He finally got the joke.

27. A Nagging Feeling

Somehow, during the night, *Loach* found itself back up on Toby's bedroom wall. A few days later Author made an appearance with an Epilogue, explaining that the giants, the river elves, and their allies had just celebrated a huge, three-day festival in *RiverHome*. On the last day, Clovor and Harold, together, removed *Loach* from the stone and replaced it with the Sword. The Sword immediately burst into life with an orange glow, lighting up the wooded area like a bonfire. *Loach,* on the other hand, seemed to be taking a long-deserved nap on Toby's wall.

But Author's Epilogue didn't bring things to an end. Occasionally, Toby would feel a sense of dread—not like his foul mood—but something that made the hairs on the back of his neck stand up. *Did he have hairs on the back of his neck?* It had to do with… Sid? Rainie? *Why Rainie?* He hadn't seen her for months. But he felt like he had. *By a waterfall?*

Then something really good happened in school. Mrs Grayson told the students that they could use their creativity in making their book reports on *Of Mice and Men*. Toby had no idea what to do at first. But as he was re-reading a *Spider-Man* comic book, an idea popped into his mind, reminding him of the pop weasels at the *Tikvah Mountains*. He shuddered at the memory. He talked with his parents about it, and they agreed that he could purchase an app for making comic books.

For the next several days, he focused all of his energy on that project. He enjoyed it so much he hadn't played a video game the entire time. Two weeks later, when he presented his comic book version of *Of Mice and Men,* his classmates applauded and oohed and aahed over it. Especially the part he added in about a mice invasion. Mrs Grayson gave him a B+. He had never had a grade that high before in English Lit. The only reason he didn't get an A was because he had a few too many spelling errors.

Grammar. Spelling. Ugh! As long as you speak good. Or is it speak well?

Maybe this was something he was good at. Even Derrick said it didn't stink. That Derrick said anything somewhat positive at all to Toby was a good thing.

Then, his band director gave him a trumpet solo for the spring concert.

And he scored the winning basket for his church's basketball team's last game of the season—albeit their only win of the year.

His counselor praised him for the hard work he had been doing in focusing on the GOOD and released Toby from counseling, assuring him that he could always call if he needed a reboot.

But underlying it all—that nagging feeling that Sid and Rainie might be in danger. He asked Author about it when Author came back with an addendum—*whatever that is*—to the Epilogue, but Author simply nodded and wrote a note in his journal.

As the school year slowly moved toward summer break, the Principal announced that the 7th graders would be spending a day at Minnehaha Falls for some fun and a bit of science. Toby's family often had picnics there with his cousins during the summer. He especially loved running down the stream to the Mississippi River and skipping rocks.

The night before the school trip, Toby's parents celebrated their 15th Wedding Anniversary with a special Sunday Pizza and Movie Night. Normally Pizza and Movie Night took place on Friday. But this was a special occasion. Grandma Baxter joined them to watch one of Toby's parents' favorite movies.

After the movie, as he was getting ready for bed, Toby noticed a sealed envelope sticking out from under his bedroom closet.

The envelope read:

An Invitation

Inside was a card:

Phoenix and Roxie Request

That you save the date

For their upcoming wedding

Toby turned the card over, looking for a date. Nothing. Then again, how could he save the date when the time in *RiverHome* didn't match the time in his world?

He placed the invite on his desk and climbed into bed. Excited as he was about the school trip in the morning, he felt that familiar nagging. Something bad was about to happen. He was sure of it. It took him a while to fall asleep. When he finally did, he had nightmares about Sid and Rainie.

On the other side of his closet, another envelope sat on the floor, too thick to squeeze under the closet door. It began to buzz. It began to glow. But then, sensing the portal opening behind it, it fell silent. The intruder didn't see it. But as he eased the closet door open slightly, he did see Toby Baxter, sound asleep.

He smiled and slid back into the closet. This was not going to be a good day for Toby Baxter.

Apparently not The End.

Toby will be back in a new adventure:

EyeHeart RiverHome

Book 4: EyeHeart RiverHome (Excerpt)

Is This a Kissing Book?

Normally Pizza and Movie Night in the Baxter household takes place on Friday. But since Toby's parents were celebrating their 15th Wedding Anniversary on Sunday, they wanted to watch their favorite movie with Toby to celebrate. So Sunday Pizza and Movie Night it was. Apparently their favorite movie was one they had watched over and over again when they were dating. On something called *Blu-ray?* They started the party early because Toby had a big day coming up on Monday: the end-of-the-school-year trip to Minnehaha Falls.

 Grandma Baxter joined them. Turns out she was also a big fan of this particular movie. Once the pizza was delivered, they settled in to watch *The Princess Bride.* Toby was pretty sure, with a title like that, that it was going to be one of those syrupy romance or rom-com chick flicks. But Grandma Baxter assured him that he would love it.

 The movie started out with a grandpa visiting his grandson, who was sick, in bed, and missing a school day. Grandpa offered to read him a story called *The Princess Bride.* And like Toby, the boy in the movie didn't seem all that excited about it. It didn't get any better as Grandpa read the opening paragraphs of the book. A girl named Buttercup liked to order the farm boy, Wesley, to do her bidding. Wesley always responded with a smile and said, "As you wish."

Buttercup soon discovered that whenever Wesley said, "As you wish," he really meant, "I love you." And Buttercup found she loved him, too.

Toby started to squirm. His gut instinct proved right. This was going to be one of those sappy love stories.

As Grandpa was about the read the next line, his grandson stopped him and asked exactly what Toby was thinking, "Wait. Is this a kissing book?"

Dad intentionally paused the movie at that point and kissed Toby's mom.

Gross!

"Toby, did we ever tell you about that time I was dropping Jan off at her parents' house after a date, and we sat in the car talking? And Jan's dad came out, in his pajamas, turned on the hose, leaned up against the car, and started watering the lawn? It must have been what, honey, 11:30 at night?"

"Only a zillion times," Toby muttered. But he always found the story pretty funny.

"Thomas," Jan said. "We'll never finish the movie if you keep interrupting it with dating stories." She leaned into his shoulder, kissed him on the cheek, and hit the play button on the remote.

Yuck!

When the movie was done, Toby had to admit that he didn't hate it. In fact, he loved it. Funny. Great one-liners. Entertaining. Lots of action. And even the kissing wasn't awful. The movie kissing that is. Mom and Dad's kissing was disgusting.

Thomas drove Grandma Baxter home, and Toby headed to his room to get ready for his school trip. The 7th graders would be spending a day at Minnehaha Falls for some fun and a bit of science. Toby's family often had picnics there with his cousins during the summer. He especially loved running down the stream to the Mississippi River and skipping rocks.

As he was about to turn off the lights and call it a night, Toby noticed a sealed envelope sticking out from under his bedroom closet. He reached down and picked it up.

The envelope read:

An Invitation

Inside was a card:

Phoenix and Roxie Request

That you save the date

For their upcoming wedding

Toby turned the card over, looking for a date. Nothing. Then again, how could he save the date when the time in *RiverHome* didn't match the time in his world? It was a timey-wimey thing.

He was excited for Phoenix and Roxie. In *RiverHome* time, they'd been together for a long time. But there would probably be lots of kissing at the wedding! *Ick!*

He placed the invite on his desk and climbed into bed. Excited as he was about the school trip in the morning, he felt a familiar nagging. Like something bad was about to happen. The nag had been nagging him since his last visit to *RiverHome*. It took him a while to fall asleep. When he finally did, he had nightmares about his friend Sid, and Rainie, a girl Toby liked.

On the other side of his closet, another envelope sat on the floor, too thick to squeeze under the closet door. It began to buzz. But then, sensing the portal opening behind it, fell silent. The intruder didn't see it. But as he eased the closet door open slightly, he did see Toby, sound asleep.

He smiled and slid back into the closet. This was not going to be a good day for Toby Baxter.

To keep up with Toby and his river elf friends, join the Toby Baxter email list at TimWrightBooks.Substack.com. You'll receive a free download of the Toby Baxter Prequel: *I.C.E. Call Toby Baxter;* the Book 2 Prequel*: Twas the Night Before RiverHome,* and the Prequel to book 3: *Not So GOOD in RiverHome.* And you will always be the first to know when Toby heads out on his next adventure.

Please support the on-going recovery efforts on Maui through the Hawaii Community Foundation.

To keep up with all of Toby's adventures, go to www.TimWrightBooks.com.

Made in the USA
Monee, IL
29 September 2024

66435379R00125